SAVE ME

A STEPBROTHER ROMANCE

BELLA SCULLY

ISBN: 151464309X
ISBN-13: 978-1514643099

DEDICATION

This book is dedicated to you, the reader.

TABLE OF CONTENTS

ACKNOWLEDGMENTS

This book would not be possible without the endless support, pep talks, and patience from my writers group.

A big thank you to all of you.

CHAPTER 1

I knew three things about Callum Gatlin:

First, he was an asshole. He radiated hate. Fifth grade inducted him into my asshole hall of fame when he tripped me at lunch, sending me flying into a splattered pool of creamed corn on the floor; little me bawled her eyes out until the office sent her home. In eighth grade, he ended my blossoming band career by stuffing a condom (unused, thank God) into my trumpet. And during junior prom last year, he snatched my corsage. I found it the next day stuffed down the

1

pants of the mascot in our lobby, forming a suggestive bulge.

Of course, I wasn't special. Cal Gatlin had his own brand of asshole for everyone, from teachers to his father to the policeman that patrolled our school halls (because of him, according to the rumor mill).

But the point still stood. Cal Gatlin had it out for everyone.

Including me.

The second rule of Cal Gatlin was that he was trouble. A criminal. Dangerous. Endless rumors surrounded him, every one of them more horrific than the last. "Did you hear Cal Gatlin set fire to the bar down the road?" "His tattoos are gang signs. My cousin said he got into the Hell's Angels." "I heard he beat his mom to death, I swear to God." If the asshole personality wasn't enough to get me to avoid him, his promising future as a prison drug smuggler was.

Third and worst of all?

As of 1PM yesterday during a tearful (then furious, then bargaining, then resigned and depressing) conversation with my mother at the kitchen table...

Callum Gatlin was my new stepbrother.

I glared at the slats of the air conditioning vent on my bedroom ceiling. The pink and purple boy band posters plastered around it smirked at me, laughing at my pain with their too-white teeth and too-blue eyes. I wondered if the vent was sharp enough to slit my wrists.

"For God's sake, Nat," Mom's voice snapped through the door, her voice echoing through the massive hallway. "Don't be such a drama queen. You and I both know we need this."

"Really, Mom? James Gatlin? Really?"

"He's a good man."

"His son sure as hell isn't."

"Natalie Amelia Harlow, you will not use profanity in this house."

My groan was muffled by feather stuffing as I smashed my down pillow over my face. I was tired of being a goody-two-shoes. I was tired of being the overachieving, obedient child, the one who made straight A's and had a 5.0 GPA. The one who never caused trouble for her single mother and always flossed after brushing. For once in my life, I wanted to act like my 17-year-old high school girl self.

And I was doing a great job at it if I say so myself.

"You said you weren't serious," I moaned into the pillow. "You said you didn't want to get remarried right away. You said you wanted to wait after Dad."

"Well, things change."

Mom's voice was tight. She hated when I used Dad against her. Even if their marriage had been rocky (and that was an extremely charitable way to describe the dumpster fire we called a home life), it wasn't fair to bring a dead man into this.

"And we need help with the house payment. James

makes me happy, Nat. And James and I need each other—we're both single parents raising teenagers. It's hard. It's lonely."

"So you decide to make it harder by marrying someone you barely know?"

"James and I have known each other for a while. We're just taking a chance for once."

"And who cares what happens to me, right?"

"Natalie, it would mean a lot if you at least tried to pretend to be okay with this. For me."

I didn't answer. Mom groaned.

"If not for me, then do it for your father."

I crawled to the door, leaning my head against it, letting my eyes sink closed. It was true. As much as I hated it, this brave carrying on is exactly what Dad would want.

And I missed him. I missed him more fiercely than anything I had ever lost in my life. I had been holding his hand when he died. Sometimes I still felt the ghost of his warm pulse on my hand, reliving the horror of its faint beat fading until only a cold emptiness remained.

Something in me died along with him. Ever since, I was a zombie. Not living, just going through the motions, terrified that somebody would realize I wasn't the perfect daughter, Student Council member, and Harvard prospect they believed me to be. Being perfect was my mask, the one I hid the pain and nightmares and migraines behind. Everybody bought it.

Except Mom. Because she felt the same pain too.

"He would want us to do this. To try to move on."

"I know, Mom," I whispered.

"Can I come in now?"

I huffed, but I reached up and turned the lock on the door. Mom pressed it open with her shoe and peeked in. Her expression softened behind her soft blonde curls. For the first time, I noticed the gray strands threading through her golden hair and how deep the wrinkles around her eyes were getting.

"Do you really want to do this?" I rasped, wiping away a tear with the back of my hand. "Shake up our lives again? We've been through too much already."

"I know, sweetie." She knelt down and wrapped her arms around me, smelling of her usual cheap rose perfume and the printing ink of the newspaper she worked at. I buried my nose in her arm, wishing I could evaporate. "We have. But maybe this is our chance. Maybe this time everything will finally get better."

"Better," I echoed, my voice bare and hollow.

"Your father would have wanted you to be happy. You know that."

"I do know, Mom. I'm just wondering how the hell rooming with Callum Gatlin is going to make things better."

"Watch your language. And who cares if James' son is troubled? Everybody is."

"He's an asshole."

She pinched me for cussing, but then drew me closer into her embrace.

"He has problems. But so does everybody. That's what family is for—taking broken people and putting them back together."

I hated that my Mom always dished out Oprah-style homegrown wisdom about Family and Love and Other Diabetes-Sweet Homey Topics. Especially because she was always irritatingly right.

She kissed my forehead.

"Just give him a chance? Give us a chance?"

I stuck my lower lip out, milking my one indulgent trip into immaturity for all it was worth. She rolled her eyes.

"For me?" Mom asked, combing her nails through my hair. "Will you give this a chance for me?"

I frowned. My throat burned, my eyes were hideously puffy and red, and the last thing I wanted to do was share a house (or worse, a bathroom—ugh) with resident town delinquent Callum Gatlin. But I could never say no to Mom when she used her sweet voice.

And I couldn't say no to her now, not if Mr. Gatlin made her happy. Mom had been so worn down since Dad's death. I glanced from the dark circles under her eyes to the fingernails she bit to stubs. Even if I was a selfish, immature child, I wouldn't let her kill herself over one of my tantrums.

"All right, Mom." I sighed one last time, making it

extra dramatic. "For you."

"Good." She kissed my forehead. "Now help me clean out the guest room. I doubt your brother will want to sleep on the couch."

Ugh.

Brother.

I picked myself up, ignoring the growing headache that threatened to split my skull, and followed her downstairs.

I had one month. One month until Cal Gatlin moved in. One month until he started the inevitable quest to bring about my mental breakdown. One month until our house would be filled with the smell of him and the sound of police sirens. One month, and my whole life would be turned upside down.

I took a deep breath.

One month.

Here goes nothing.

CHAPTER 2

The month passed in an instant.

Mom and Mr. Gatlin—who insisted I call him James every time he visited for dinner, flashing his white veneered smile—opted for a small courthouse wedding. I wore a navy lace dress Mom picked out for me from one of the thrift shops around the block. Mr. Gatlin (or, James, I guess) bought her silk violets for her bouquet. The ceremony lasted fifteen minutes.

Callum didn't come.

Thank God.

But he couldn't stay out of my life forever. A week after they pulled away from the courthouse with a tiny placard reading "just married" taped to the rear window, the U-Haul vans arrived. I sat on the front lawn, picking nervously at the skirt of my pink sundress as each one dragged old furniture and cartons of books into the house.

I kept out of the way, dodging any sign of Cal Gatlin.

Or at least I tried to.

My plan didn't last long. Because the last U-Haul carried not only more boxes and a futon from the 80s, but Cal Gatlin.

"Hey, Sis."

Cal was leaning against the truck, ignoring the few relatives hauling in the last pieces of furniture. I flinched. I had avoided him since the last prom incident aside from a few glares from him in the hallway.

I guess my luck had to run out at some point.

Since then, he had grown at least a few inches on his already tall frame. Now he towered over me like a hulking giant. The constant fighting had paid off in muscles that rippled across his arms. Tight abs stretched his shirt, and new tattoos and scars laced across his strong arms. A single diamond stud glittered in his left ear as bright as the two green eyes that fell on me with a smirk.

My stomach turned as my gaze traveled down to that smirk.

Glaring I could handle. With glaring, I knew where we stood. He hated me for being the blonde goody-goody to his dark bad boy. As long as we avoided each other, we would avoid conflict. Smiling was something horrifically worse, one that made my eyes widen and my lip tremble.

Smiling meant Cal Gatlin was happy to see me. Smiling meant I was Cal Gatlin's new toy.

The hair on my neck rose as his smirk grew.

"Don't call me that," I snapped. "I am not your Sis."

Cal's lip curled. "What's wrong, Sis? Ashamed of your family?"

"Shut up," I snapped.

Heat crept up my cheeks as they burned bright red. My pink, cardigan-addicted pianist self was no match for Cal Gatlin, and I knew it. I wanted run to bed and crawl under the covers and forget this ever happened.

Please, God, let me fall asleep tonight and wake up and realize it was all a dream. Dad would be alive and reading the paper at the kitchen table. Mom would be mixing her Sunday morning pancakes at the counter. I'd walk downstairs and tell them what a crazy dream I'd had that Mom would marry someone like James Gatlin, and they'd laugh and laugh.

I picked myself up and trudged indoors, keeping my gaze fixed ahead of me.

Don't look at him.

Don't look at him.

Don't look at him.

Shit, I looked.

My heart fluttered into my throat. Out of the corner of my eye, Cal Gatlin was stalking after me. His leather jacket stretched tight over his broad shoulders, his ripped jeans hugging the muscular legs that had tripped me when I was a kid in middle school. I hated him. I hated his earring, his smirk, the forest green eyes that tracked me like a cat preying on a mouse.

"Where're you going, Sis? Don't you want to spend some quality time with your big brother?"

"Shut the f—"

I halted as Mom and James walked out of the kitchen, blissfully unaware that their daughter was being stalked by her potential murderer. Cal's smirk grew, and he crossed the room with wide strides. I stood frozen at the steps of the stairs.

Please, God, let Mom bury me somewhere nice.

"What's wrong, Sis?" He tilted his head, and that predatory, toothy smile spread as his full lips parted. "Can't use big bad grown up words in front of Mommy and Daddy? Maybe I should teach you a few."

"Gatlin, I don't get what the fuck you're doing—"

"There. That's a good one. Fuck." His hand reached over my shoulder to prop himself against the wall. He leaned forward, the heat rolling off his body in waves against mine. He had me pinned with no escape

12

route. My blue eyes grew wider. "You know what fuck means, Sis?"

I froze. His body was too close to mine, his gaze too intense. The word fuck hung in the air between us, teasing me.

His smirk grew as my silence held. "That's okay, Sis. I'll have lots of time to teach you about fuck. I can teach you about fuck all day." His eyes raked down my body again, making me shiver. My heart pounded in my throat. "Let's see. How about cock? That's a nice, big grown up word. Cock."

I flinched. The word cock rolled off so easily from his full lips. Every inch of my body was electric and breathless. Fight or flight was kicking in.

"Fuck off, Gatlin," I breathed.

"Mm, good, you've learned fuck. But how about a big word like cock? How big do you like it, Sis?" He leaned forward again, his nose an inch from mine. His glittering green eyes burned a hole into mine, his smirk growing poisonous. "Go on, we're family. You can tell your big brother anything. Tell your big brother how big you like cock."

"I told you to fuck off."

"Say it after me. Let me see it come out of those pretty little lips. Cock."

"You're disgusting."

In the bravest moment of my life, I pressed my hands against Cal's chest and shoved as hard as I could.

His eyes grew wide, and he stumbled back, more out of shock than force. The boy was hard as rock and weighed a ton, and my hands felt feeble against him.

"Don't. Ever. Touch me. Again," I spat.

I willed my voice to sound strong. His eyes widened. A strange expression flashed across his face. Was it … respect?

Impossible. The only thing Cal Gatlin respected was himself.

"I didn't touch you," he grunted.

"Like hell you didn't."

"I leaned over you. Leaning ain't touching, Sis. Though trust me. I'd love to touch."

I suppressed the bile rising in my throat and marched up the stairs. Count to ten, Nat. Count to ten, do some mindfulness exercises, do whatever you have to, just don't engage him. Do not encourage Cal Gatlin, because the one thing Cal Gatlin loves is prey that fights back.

Unable to stop myself, I glanced over to see Cal still leaning against the wall, his eyes raking my body again.

"What are you—are you undressing me with your eyes?" I choked.

"Can't help liking what I see."

I clutched my coat around me as if that would help.

He smirked.

"What's wrong, Sis?" He leaned forward, his eyes searching mine again. "Afraid I'm not giving it enough credit? Want to give me a firsthand taste?"

"God, you're revolting!"

"See, I already have you screaming. I bet you'd scream louder in bed."

"Callum!"

"Mm. Like that. Say my name a little more."

I gagged and scrambled up the stairs. My foot caught the last step, sending me stumbling, and the sound of Cal's dark chuckle followed. My eyes burned with tears. I had to get into my bedroom before he saw my expression. I couldn't let him win. His footsteps thudded closer, and I darted into my room before he cornered me again.

I slammed the door, rattling the frame viciously.

The simultaneous voices of my mother and James yelled up at me to cut it out. I grimaced. If James was already feeling bold enough to yell at me, that did not bid well for my hopes he would get intimidated and run.

The soft ruffling of paper sounded through the door. Then a moment of silence. I jumped as a folded note slipped under the door and rested at my feet.

Cal's deep voice chuckled again as his footsteps padded away to his new room.

I waited until he was gone to unfold it and read:

If you want to scream, you know where to find me. Cum on over, Sis.

My fingers trembled around the note, my body shaking in anger. Sure, a moron like Cal Gatlin had no idea how to spell, but something told me that he very much meant it when he asked me to cum. I crushed it into a ball and threw it into the pink wastebasket next to my desk.

Callum Gatlin thought he was would beat me, I thought as I fell into bed, pulling a pillow over my head to dry the tears.

Callum Gatlin was fucking wrong.

CHAPTER 3

Cal and his father moved in on a Sunday. Which was great, because I would have gone crazy being around him for an entire weekend.

Instead, I skipped dinner that night by pretending to be asleep when Mom checked in at six ("Oh, poor thing, she's just so tired. It's been a big day, James"). I doubted someone like Cal was civilized enough to eat at the table like a human being, but I wasn't taking any chances.

On the bright side, Cal never made it less than an

hour late to school, which meant I didn't have to worry about my morning routine. I pulled on a pink sweater, scooped my hair into a bun, and made a break for my bike before the light underneath his door had even flicked on.

The weight of the world lifted from my shoulders as I pulled into the school's parking lot. My once shaking, now calm hands chained my bike up, and I strolled into the cafeteria with a smile on my face. Free at last.

Or at least that's what I thought.

"It's not true, is it?" Jess stage whispered from behind me. "Jesus—Cal Gatlin, really?"

My smile disappeared.

My best friend—the brunette to my blonde, the VP to my President, the yin to my yang—fell into step beside me the second I pushed through the school's front doors. Stares and whispers followed me everywhere today, but somehow hers were louder than all the rest combined.

I gritted my teeth. Regardless of how preppy I dressed, how fine I acted, or how early I showed up, the stench of Callum Gatlin clung to me, turning heads wherever I went.

"Really," I muttered. I pulled my hoodie over my face, hoping to hide until this all died down.

"God, what's it like living with him?"

"Disgusting. He's absolutely disgusting."

"Come on, Sis, I need details."

"Don't call me Sis," I snapped, my voice a little too passionate. Her face twisted.

"Oh God, does he call you that?"

I pursed my lips, and she gasped.

"Jesus Christ, Nat."

"Yeah, well, I'm banking on him getting expelled or arrested before anything gets too bad." I pulled the hoodie tighter over me as a gaggle of teachers paused their chatter to sneak glances. Ugh. Even the faculty knew I was a dead woman. "Until then, I'm camping out at your place."

"Aw, not mine?" a voice said behind me as an arm looped over my shoulder.

My boyfriend (yes, I should mention I have a boyfriend—do you see now why this situation was so shit?) slid his arm around me. His name was Nathaniel, but everybody called him Nate, and sometimes I think the only reason we got pushed together was that Nat and Nate sounded too cute together.

That, and the fact that he was my only competition for valedictorian, he was the president of just as many clubs as I was, and lacrosse practice and swim meets had made him attractive. Enough teachers playing matchmaker and comments from Jess about singleness not fitting the perfect overachiever image later, we were dating.

If you could call sticking our tongues down each other's throats at football games "dates."

"You're probably right, anyway," Nate said. "Dicks like Gatlin never graduate. I heard he was failing every class, even shop."

Nate clapped me on the back. His hand was a little too low this time, brushing the top of my ass. I grimaced. He had gotten handsy lately, despite my protests.

"Yeah, well," I grumbled, slipping into homeroom, "if I don't make it to lunch, you'll know who murdered me."

I wasn't murdered, though, because Cal didn't show up to first period—or second, or third, or fourth. The stares and whispers grew, but they became bearable when I realized that they were sympathetic.

And impressed. People weren't just amazed that someone like Cal was related to someone like me, they were amazed I had survived the night. A few teachers pulled me aside to offer assistance, and I noticed the hall cop keeping a protective eye on me. I was a war hero returning from the battlefield.

Maybe I really would make it.

By lunch, I was feeling positively cheery.

That hope was dashed to pieces when I sat down between Nate and Jess with my brown bagged lunch. Across the cafeteria, the doors burst open with a sharp kick. My mouth went dry as Cal stepped in, his eyes scanning the fields of students. They landed on me, and his face lit up with a smirk.

"Hide me," I squawked at Jess.

"Don't be such a drama queen," Jess said. Her voice was shaking. Even if everybody looked down on Cal, they were still rightfully terrified of him. "He's your brother."

"Stepbrother! Step!"

She mumbled something at me as I plotted my escape routes. But a shadow cast over me. Jess went silent.

From behind me, right in my ear:

"Aw, come on, Sis. Don't be like that."

He drew the word Sis out nice and long, letting it hiss off of his tongue. Cal stood behind me, his hands on either side of my chair, the warmth of his body pressing against my back. He grabbed Nate's chair, currently vacant, and pulled it out with a squeal. He fell into it with a thump, and his green eyes fixed on me.

"You look sick, Sis. Need some TLC?"

"You can't sit here."

"Sorry, princess, this ain't Mean Girls." He leaned forward. "Besides, your mother said we need to spend some quality time together. We need to bond."

His hand rested on my knee, and every joint in my body locked.

Please go away, please go away, please go away.

"Aren't you afraid Officer Furst will find you?" I snapped, hoping the looming threat of prison would scare him off.

He snorted. "Please. Furst doesn't have anything on me." He leaned forward, his smirk even more threatening. "I'm too good at covering my tracks."

"Just go away," I groaned, pinching the bridge of my nose.

His gaze burned into me again, and I swore I would have a talk with my mother about this. Then again, I doubted she would listen to me. His grip on my knee tightened, snapping me back to reality. The reality where Cal Gatlin was leaning forward and asking me if I needed help to do anything naughty with a twinkle in his eyes.

"And anyway—" Cal continued.

"Get your hands off my girlfriend."

Nate's harsh voice rose from behind us. With a lazy grimace, Cal glanced over his shoulder. Nate stood there, his hands balled into fists, glaring hard enough to kill someone. For once, I was glad I had a boyfriend. Nate could be possessive, but maybe that was a good thing sometimes.

"Why?"

"She doesn't want you here."

"She hasn't made me move yet." Cal's smirk grew, and his head cocked to the side, letting the diamond stud glitter. "Afraid she likes me more than you, pretty boy?"

"Cal, fuck off," I snapped. "Nate, lose the fists."

Cal's eyes glanced at me, studying my expression.

Nate, as usual, ignored me, his hands trembling with anger.

"You've got five seconds, Gatlin."

"Nate," I said.

"Til what?" Cal leaned forward, his eyes mockingly wide. "I told you. She wants me here."

"Like hell she does. Two seconds, Gatlin."

"Til what?" he repeated. "Til you hit me like you hit her?"

Shit. Don't say that!

It was too late. Nate's eyes were already on fire.

Nate lurched forward, swinging his fists at my new stepbrother. I stood up so fast to stop him that my chair squealed back, echoing throughout the cafeteria.

Every head in the room turned to us, no longer pretending to give us our privacy. I hated when Nate acted like this—like I couldn't handle myself, like I was his property. Even if Cal Gatlin was a menace, I didn't need him causing a scene.

"Nate, stop," I hissed, grabbing his arm.

Without considering the hundreds and hundreds of eyes that were on us, Nate threw his arm back, shoving me away from him. I stumbled and fell on my ass, my chest aching where he had shoved me. My lungs gasped for the air that he had knocked out of them.

Nate was stronger than he realized. Or at least that's the excuse I gave him, ignoring all the other times it had happened.

Everyone fixed their eyes on the impending brawl above me, too distracted to notice my place on the ground. Thank God, I thought, rubbing the sore spot where he had shoved me.

"Don't fucking hurt her!" Cal growled. My eyes grew wide as he lurched forward and grabbed Nate by the shoulders.

Oh God, he's going to kill him. He's going to kill him and I'm going to have to testify at the trial.

Nate had no chance against him, and everybody knew it. He was fit, but in a lithe, swimmer kind of way. No match for Cal's street fighting muscles.

Luckily, Nate didn't need chance.

He needed a three hundred pound hall monitor.

At that moment, our hulking school police officer, Officer Furst, burst through the crowd surrounding them. He grabbed Cal's shoulders and ripped him away from Nate. Furst was the only person in the town stronger than Cal, which was probably why he was assigned to our high school.

Cal knew it too, but that wasn't going to stop him from putting up a fight. He drew his hand back to punch Furst from the side.

"Please, don't," I whispered from my pathetic place on the floor.

Cal's gaze flitted toward me one more time. I had no idea what I had expected. Cal Gatlin had no reason to listen to me. He hated me and everything I stood for, from my cream cardigans to the National Honor Society pin on my floral backpack. He should have ignored me.

Instead, his eyes stayed fixed on me, burning into me. It was a strange gaze. There was something more there, something I couldn't figure out.

Was Cal feeling protective of his new sister?

His fists dropped immediately.

Even Furst's eyes widened, unused to this new pacifism. I watched Furst march Cal away, the eyes of the entire cafeteria mercifully off of me and onto them.

"I told you he was a dick," Nate growled, grabbing his seat and falling into it.

Jess grabbed my hand, pulling me up from the floor. Nate kept his gaze fixed on his backpack as he ripped his homework out of it. He didn't look at me.

The sounds of cafeteria chatter flooded back as people lost interest in us. I stared at my peanut butter sandwich while Jess restored the natural order by babbling on about Vanessa Miller From Homeroom's new haircut. Just five minutes, and everything was back to normal.

Well, everything except the pain in my chest.

The image of Cal's intense gaze burned in my mind. Why had he looked at me like that? Why had he listened to me when I asked him to stop? Was I right about my guess that Cal was beginning to feel protective of me, regardless of how stupid and unreasonable the relationship between us was? My stomach turned.

I frowned and looked down at my lunch.

No. There was no way.

Cal and I were not connected at all. The best thing to do was keep pretending he didn't exist.

CHAPTER 4

Nate, as usual, offered me a ride home.

And as usual, I smiled and said no.

Instead I stayed late after school to run club meetings and steal an hour in the piano practice room. By the time the sunset glowed golden pink and the school's clock tower was chiming six, I was sure I was in the clear. There was no way I would run into Cal. By now he was home, cooped up in his room, skulking or setting fires or building pipe bombs or whatever he did for fun.

I threw on my backpack and slipped out the front doors of the school, shutting the lights of the back room off behind me for the cleaning ladies. My feet hit the pavement of the sidewalk with a cheery little jump, celebrating my new freedom from stupid, hormonal teenage boys. Dinner waited for me at home. And then the stack of glorious, glorious homework on my desk promised to keep my mind off the criminal in the bedroom next to me.

"Hey, Sis."

My skin prickled.

Shit.

I kept walking but turned my head. Cal Gatlin was strolling behind me, his scuffed boots and leather jacket looking as beaten up as always, his smirk as irritating as ever.

"Why are you still here?" I snapped.

My fingers clutched the backpack strap and pulled it closer as if that protected me. Pepper spray was going on my to-buy list this weekend.

"I had detention, didn't you hear? They made me stay after."

"I thought detention ended at five thirty?"

"And I thought my new little sister could use an escort home. I stayed after for you, Sis. Aren't you special?"

"It's a miracle they let you out at all," I grumbled. "You almost clocked a police officer."

"Didn't you hear? I managed not to punch him. Pulled back at the last minute. I'm 'growing as a moral actor.' Aren't you proud, Sis?"

I didn't answer. I didn't understand what Cal Gatlin was after, and I didn't care. My headache was pulsing against my temples, and I ached for my bed and homework. Please, God, let this be a nightmare.

Yet something was eating away at me. Something in the way he had looked at me, the way he had stopped when I asked him to earlier. And I was sure as hell it wasn't because Cal Gatlin was becoming a 'moral actor.'

Still, I kept walking. I refused to turn around and face him.

Gatlin fell into step with me, and I flinched. Please go away, please go away, please go away.

"So, you broke up with pretty boy yet?"

"Nate is a good boyfriend." I gritted my teeth.

Please go away, please go away, please go away.

He snorted. "Didn't seem so good when he shoved you on your ass."

"I wonder why that happened. Couldn't be that anybody was egging him on."

"Oh, really? Getting egged on is an excuse to hit your girlfriend? Damn, Pink, nobody told me."

I gritted my teeth. No, fuck this. Forget what happened earlier. He was back to being an asshole. If I was smart, I would remember that that's what Cal always was.

"Fuck. Off. Cal."

"Cal? Are we that close already that we're giving each other nicknames, Pink?"

I ignored him. Do not encourage him, I reminded myself. Do not let yourself become Cal Gatlin's new toy. I hugged my jacket closer and kept walking.

"Come on, Sis. Don't you want to get all close and intimate? Get inside each other's head?" His gaze scraped my body again. "Bad boy and good girl, best friends forever? It could happen."

"This isn't the Breakfast Club. And I'm not Molly Ringwald. Fuck off."

His eyebrows raised, and a cocky grin played across his face.

"Damn, Sis. I love a chick with a mouth. Glad I married you."

"You didn't marry me. My mother married your father. For some reason."

"You do have a nice mouth."

"Shut up."

"I wonder what else you can do with it."

My face burned crimson, and I ducked. Yes, he was back to being good old Cal Gatlin, the boy who humiliated me in third grade. The boy who had it out for me for some strange reason.

Why, God, why did Mom have to marry James? Couldn't they act like the Baby Boomer hippies they were and decide marriage was just a piece of paper? Or choose to live separately? Or at least sell Cal to the zoo or something.

"You can quit pretending you don't want me," he said, slinking along beside me. "I've seen your type before, Pink. Bad boys get you wet."

"Don't talk to me."

"Is that why you fuck douchebags like Nate, hm?"

"I haven't fucked him," I blurted.

Oh God, that was the wrong choice. My heart sank as soon as Cal turned his head, his smirk gleaming in the setting sunlight.

"So you really are a good girl, Pink? You're a virgin?"

"Shut up."

"Has nobody popped your cherry yet?"

"Shut up."

"You need help with that?"

I sped up. He fell into step with me again instantly. I'd never be fast enough evade him, not with my short little legs and his cocky determination. He stuck to me like a leech.

"That's all right, Sis. I like the view from behind better, anyway."

I whirled on him. "Seriously, Gatlin, can you just leave? I don't know what you want from me, but you're not getting it."

"Gatlin? We're not on nickname basis anymore, Pink?"

"I told you to leave."

"I'm walking home. To our home."

Ugh. It was our home, and there was nothing I could do about that.

"You don't have to be such an ass, Cal. I told you. I don't get what you want, besides getting a rise out of me."

"It's only fair, baby. You've definitely gotten a rise out of me." The way he drew out the word rise made me shiver.

He chuckled.

"I saw that, Pink. I told you: girls like you always want bad boys. It's in your blood. Anyway, you know exactly what I want."

"And what's that?" I spat.

"You."

"Then you're sure as hell not getting it."

My footsteps sped up. Our house rose ahead of us as Cal babbled on, attempting to provoke a response out of me. I tuned it out, squeezing my eyes shut as I entered the house and peeled off my coat.

Don't be his new toy. Don't encourage him.

I ignored Mom's calls from the kitchen to come to dinner, instead heading for my room. Cal trailed after me, his voice rising an octave as he realized that I was about to escape him.

"Come on, Pink. You've got something to say. I can feel it. Just say it."

"Leave me alone, Gatlin. I've told you everything I need to say."

"That's not true. Remember our conversation yesterday? You haven't told me how big you like cock."

"You're disgusting."

"Is that why you're still a virgin? Pretty boy not big enough for you?"

My patience broke, and I sprinted for the stairs. I couldn't handle him anymore. I didn't care if he listened to me at lunch, I didn't care if he didn't kill Nate, I didn't care that for a moment he had seemed human.

Today was a lesson. I couldn't trust Cal Gatlin. No matter how "good" he seemed from one moment, he would be an absolute dick the next.

I hated him, I hated him, I hated him.

"Fuck off, Cal. I'm sick of you."

"Oh, please. You don't care. You're too busy being perfect."

I gritted my teeth and balled my fists.

Don't encourage him, Nat.

"Natalie Harlow, the perfect little girl," he sneered. "You know why I like fucking with you?" He leaned against the wall, glaring a hole into me. "Because you're sick of me. Because you're ashamed of me."

Don't answer, don't encourage him, don't let yourself be his new toy.

"You are ashamed, aren't you?" He barked a laugh.

"Ashamed to be related to me. I fuck up your perfect little life. You hate it."

"I'm not perfect," I rasped.

"Please. So fucking perfect. You're a real fucking Miss Congeniality, aren't you? So smart, so pretty, so virginal. You've never had a problem in your life."

"Fuck off, Cal!" I exploded at him. "Just do everyone a favor and fuck off!"

My mother's voice shouted at me from the kitchen, and I could hear her light footsteps chasing after me. I flew up the stairs before she could meet me. Tears stung my eyes.

"Come on, Sis." His voice was acidic. "Let's spend some quality time together."

"Nate's right, you know," I said, whirling on him when I reached the stop of the stairs. "You're a huge dick."

"Bigger than he is? I knew you liked it big. You wouldn't be able to resist me."

"Fuck off, Gatlin," I choked through the tears that burned my throat. "I don't know what you want, and I don't care."

"I want to spend time with my little sister, Sis."

"Why?" I choked over the sound of Mom's furious footsteps stomping after us. Memories of the gossip surrounding Cal flooded back, and my lip curled. "So you can beat me to death like you beat your mom?"

He froze in the hallway.

"What the fuck did you just say?"

I whirled on him. "I told you to fuck off!"

There was a blazing fire in his gaze as it fixed on me. This wasn't the usual Cal Gatlin against the world glare. This was hatred. Pure, raw hatred. He wanted to burn me to the ground.

But it evaporated in an instant.

His gaze followed a tear as it dripped down my cheek. His lips parted, and he took a step back. The glare softened in shock.

"Are you... are you crying?"

His voice halted. He was still growling, but there was something else there, a break that revealed... regret? Pain?

Maybe even sympathy?

I didn't know, and I didn't care. I turned again, marching to my room, hoping my feet came down hard enough to crack the hardwood floor.

Cal didn't follow. He stood stone still at the foot of the stairs, watching as I hurled my bag into the room. His broad shoulders leaned against the wall, his arms crossed, his irritating diamond stud gleaming in the dim light of the foyer.

But his eyes had changed. Instead of a hard glare, they had softened.

"I'm not as fucking perfect as you think," I snarled.

I slammed the door, leaving him frozen on the other side.

CHAPTER 5

At eight, Mom's fist pounded the door, ordering me to come down and eat something. At nine, James came to bargain me out with the promise of a trip to the movies, as if that was worth seeing Cal again. By ten, they both huffed and decided that I was a worthless drama queen. As they left, Mom mumbled something to James about starving me out eventually.

They were right.

At midnight, my growling stomach overtook me

with complaints about missing two dinners in a row and a breakfast on top of that. I crept downstairs, grabbed a bag of dry cereal and a banana, and flew back to my room as fast as possible. Surely I had made my getaway unseen, right?

Of course not. Cal was leaning against my open bedroom door, his arms crossed, one eyebrow raised.

"Hm," he said, his voice subdued. "I was starting to think you're anorexic."

"Fuck off, Gatlin," I groaned.

My voice was weak. I couldn't muster up the energy to bark it as an order anymore. He was winning, and he knew it, which must be why that cocky glare was missing.

"You all right?"

"As if you care."

I sidestepped him and slipped into my room, my body aching with the stress of the day. My hands pushed against the door to shut it, but Gatlin walked in after me, elbowing it open with his much stronger, tattooed arm.

Fine. Fuck it. He can stay.

I was too tired to fight with him, and I didn't have enough time to waste on him regardless. My aching body collapsed into my desk chair. I began devouring the cereal by the handful, my stomach groaning in relief.

"Damn, Pink." Gatlin sat at the edge of my bed, and I winced, sure he would get my flawlessly washed and softened comforter dirty. "You eat like a trucker."

"Look, Gatlin—"

I turned around to tell him off, but the sheer weirdness of seeing him lying in my bed struck me. His body glistened with water from the shower, his black hair slicked back behind his ears as little droplets traveled down his neck. He wore nothing but a pair of gray sweatpants, giving me a view of the tattoos that laced his muscled body and the rock-hard abs that built his stomach. Judging from the embarrassingly prominent bulge, he was also going commando.

Jesus, the boy was hung like a horse. No wonder he fixated on the word cock.

"You gonna say something, or just keep staring?"

I turned around, glaring at my day planner.

God damn him.

In a flat voice, I answered: "If you're going to make me cry again, you can just leave."

A few moments of awkward silence.

He sighed and rubbed his neck. "Look. Natalie." It was the first time he said my real name. My eyebrows raised. I kept my eyes fixed on my desk, but my ears perked.

"I… uh, I wanted to… talk about that," he said. There was something strange about his tone and the way his gaze landed on me, soft and cautious instead of hard and angry. Was he regretting what he had said earlier?

Cal Gatlin showing remorse for something? This must be a bad dream. It had to be.

"Well, I don't. The door is that way."

Cal frowned. "I didn't mean to… uh, hurt you."

I could hear his voice halting and wavering, like he was unsure of himself. Cal Gatlin being anything other than a cocky motherfucker? Impossible. But there it was.

"I wanted to…. Well, I wanted to apologize. I guess you're right—I don't know what I was after. But it wasn't making you cry. It was shitty. I'm sorry." He winced at the word sorry, like it took every bit of will to say it.

The word apologize hung in the air.

I was too in shock to respond.

"You still alive?" He raised an eyebrow at my frozen form sitting at the desk.

"Yes."

"So are we… uh, are we good?"

I didn't answer. He sighed again and rolled his eyes. But he didn't leave. Instead, he laced his fingers behind his head and laid back on my bed, resting like he was planning on sleeping there. The sight of his form stretched out like a lazy cat did strange things to me.

Wait, no. Focus, Nat. Like hell he was staying here for a second longer. I cleared my throat.

"Yes. We're good." I gritted my teeth, wincing at the memory of what I had spat at him. The shitty one liner about beating his mom. "And, uh. I'm sorry. For what I said."

He shrugged. He kept his eyes fixed on the ceiling, his expression bored and vacant. I guess he heard that kind of thing all the time. It didn't mean much coming from me too.

"You can leave now," I said.

Instead of leaving, he let his eyes wander around my room, his gaze flitting from one end to the other. He inspected the perfectly organized desk, the boy band posters plastered on the ceiling, and the pink floral wallpaper. His gaze crossed to the sticky note reminders and pictures of friends at parties and school that dotted my wall. I stared at his face, trying to figure out why he was still here.

But my gaze wandered down his body, starting at the diamond stud earring and down the thick muscles of his chest. The tempting happy trail of hair led down his sculpted stomach to a bulge in his sweatpants. I didn't like it, but my mind kept drifting back to the memory of Cal saying cock.

I swallowed.

"You really like pink, don't you, Pink?" he asked. I tore my gaze away to see him inspecting one of my embroidered pillows.

"Don't call me that."

"Why not?"

"Because I hate pink."

He paused, cocking an eyebrow. "You colorblind, then?"

I snorted. Cal? Having a sense of humor outside 'making my stepsister as embarrassingly wet as possible'?

I guess miracles do happen.

"No," I said, sitting down and opening my day planner. I had five bi-weekly meetings to plan, a bake sale to organize, and college applications to prepare for submission. I didn't have time for Callum Gatlin and whatever panty raid level bullshit he was planning. He needed to leave, and I needed to quit looking at his abs like that.

"You gonna explain this shit, then?" He jumped up and stalked toward me. I froze, watching his hand reach over my shoulder. Oh God, he was going to choke the life out of me. (And then Mom would regret marrying James, wouldn't she?)

Instead, he picked up a pink stack of stationary and glanced over the lacy doily print with distaste.

I snatched it from him.

"Because people like me are supposed to like pink. So I like pink."

"I thought you said you hated it."

"I do hate it," I answered.

He studied me as I worked, sitting on the edge of my desk, the heat of his body oddly inviting. I attempted to focus on reading through the minutes of the last Student Council meeting, but his burning green gaze was too distracting. I swallowed hard and closed my eyes, wishing more than anything my life could go back to like it was before.

"You got a problem, Sis?"

"Yeah. You. Is there a reason you're here, other than to molest me?"

His lips curled into a frown. "I never laid a finger on you."

"You touched my knee."

"Sorry, I didn't know knee-touching counted as molesting." He paused, and a devilish grin flooded his face. "Why, Sis? You want me to?"

"Oh, fuck off."

Wait, I was smiling. Why was I smiling at Cal Gatlin? He was an asshole, and the fact that he had shown a moment of empathy for once in his life didn't change that.

I forced my mouth into a hard, thin line.

"I'm proud of you, Sis. Don't think I've ever heard a chick with a mouth like yours—at least when you're not around Mommy." He sat on the edge of my desk, and the warmth of his leg teased my hand. I folded my hands into my lap and swallowed again. "Funny how you drop the good girl act when you're around me."

"Funny how you never drop the asshole act."

His mouth twitched. Now he was smiling at me. Cal Gatlin was sitting in my room, on my desk, smiling at me, and it wasn't because he was trying to murder me. What was going on?

"I meant it, Sis. I am an asshole, I won't deny that. But I'm sorry for earlier."

"If you're sorry, then don't call me Sis."

"All right. Natalie."

I turned back to my papers, all of them now a vague blur. It was so bizarre, the way he said my name. His lips wrapped around it so easily, and it rolled out as smooth as warm butter. His voice was soft and kind. Soft and kind were the last things I would ever associate with Cal Gatlin.

And most bizarre of all was the way it became more impossible to keep my eyes off of him the longer he sat next to me. I had never thought about Cal as anything other than my tormentor. So why was my heart fluttering?

"Why do you hate me?" I asked, keeping my gaze fixed on my hands.

Cal shifted in his seat, uncomfortable. "I don't hate you."

"Please. You've tormented me since I was a kid."

"Yeah, well, like I said, I'm an asshole. It doesn't mean I hate you."

"Then why? Why do you keep doing this? Why do you never leave me alone?"

He sighed and looked down, keeping his arms crossed. My gaze ran along the faded eagle tattoo that curled around his bicep. The muscles in his arm were mesmerizing, even beneath the haze of my anger at him.

I shouldn't be thinking about Cal Gatlin this way, not after the way he treated me. But something about the way he said sorry was softening me towards him.

"Because you're perfect," he said. "You've got friends. You're smart as shit. You're gorgeous." He paused. "You're everything I'm not."

My eyes widened. Gorgeous? And more importantly, Cal being jealous? Why would he ever want anything about my life? I thought he hated me and everything I stood for.

"I'm not … perfect."

"Yeah, well, you're more perfect than most people will ever be," he muttered. At that moment, my sleep shirt, a loose sweatshirt that fell off my shoulder constantly, slipped again.

His gaze wandered down to glance at the flesh of my chest before I pulled the sleeve up. I expected him to leer, but his expression was hurt instead.

I glanced down, following his eyes.

A purple bruise was blooming above my right breast, the spot where Nate had shoved me.

Cal zeroed in on it.

"Did he hurt you?" His voice was flat and dark.

"Why? You don't give a shit."

"Did. He. Hurt. You."

"That's none of your business."

Before I could stop him, Cal leaned down and touched my shoulder. I froze. The warmth of his fingertips across my skin, pulling my shirt down and resting against my neck, was electric. At first I thought I couldn't move out of fear. But then I realized I wasn't afraid of Cal, not when he was touching me so gently.

I felt safe. Safe and cared for, for the first time in a long time. To have someone acknowledge that I was wounded and want to make it better ... even if that person was Cal Gatlin, it was something I wanted to never stop. His touch wasn't forcing me still out of fear. I was still because I liked it.

"You're hurt," Cal growled. "I'll kill him."

"Cal, just drop it."

"No. This isn't the first time he's given you a bruise, is it?"

"Go away."

"How many times has he hit you? In public, even? And no one ever stops it, do they? They pretend it didn't even happen."

"Cal, please."

"Or maybe they convince themselves it didn't happen. No way the perfect kid could hurt his perfect girlfriend."

"Cal." My voice was growing weak.

"I saw it happen last year. When you two were in the parking lot a few hours after school, when you thought nobody else was around, I was there. I wanted to fucking kill him."

"Why do you care, Gatlin?"

My voice broke on the last word. Tears stung my eyes as they welled, and my hands were shaking in my lap.

"Can you quit acting like you don't know?" he said, his voice irritated. His fingers traced the blooming bruise, their touch feather light. I had no idea that Cal Gatlin, the tattooed bad boy, could be so gentle. "I know you think I'm shit. I know you'd never consider it. But quit acting like you don't know why I care. It's getting old, all right?"

"I'm not acting. Just please …." My voice broke again. I couldn't stand having him here anymore. "Leave."

Cal's fingers lingered on my skin for a second longer, and a part of my wanted him to never let go. But finally, he sighed and picked himself up, crossing his arms again. I kept my gaze fixed on the hands in my lap. I couldn't bring myself to look up at him, into his eyes. I couldn't let him see me cry again.

"You can keep pretending everything's all right, Nat," he murmured. "But you're right about one thing. Your life isn't perfect. And the more you pretend it is, the worse it's going to get."

"Cal, just go."

"I can't save you if you won't let me."

"I don't need to be saved."

"I see you," he said. "I know."

He turned for the door. His tall, dark form lingered in the doorway, then glanced at me once last time. His gaze was soft.

"When you're ready to quit acting, you know where to find me. Even if I am an asshole, I'm the only one who isn't buying your act. And I don't care if you're not perfect."

I didn't answer. Instead, I waited for the soft click of the door closing, and then dragged myself in bed.

To hell with planning for the week. I needed sleep. And I needed to suppress the warm feelings that were growing inside me, urging me to admit that he was right—my life wasn't perfect. I ached to confess that to someone.

But not Cal Gatlin. Never him.

Right?

The warmth of my blankets over me was heaven. I buried my face into the pillows, and I was met with a surprising new scent, something other than the usual scent of my strawberry shampoo.

Cal. My sheets smelled of Cal.

And I was surprised to realize it was delicious. Like smoke, the tang of motorcycle grease, the freshness of his soap and shampoo, and a deep musk that was uniquely him.

I buried my nose in my pillow, inhaling the deep, masculine musk. My muscles released and my heart slowed. I wrapped my arms around it, letting the warmth that Cal's body left on it radiate around me, coaxing me into sleep. It made me feel what I felt when he touched me earlier. Safe.

Wait, shit! What was I doing?

I groaned and threw the pillow away.

No. No, no, no.

Was I feeling … friendly towards Cal? Something more, even? How on earth could someone so annoying smell so lovely, or even make me laugh like he had just a few minutes ago? Why was I aching to grab the pillow and drown in it again?

No. I refused to even think about what that meant.

I turned over in my sleep and pulled the sheets over me. Cal and I had a truce, sure. That was all it was.

That was all it would ever be.

CHAPTER 6

The next morning, I didn't slip out of the house as fast as possible. Something kept me lingering, taking extra time to button my cardigan and lace my tennis shoes. I passed by Cal's room more than I needed to, my gaze constantly flitting to the crack underneath his door.

It stayed dark.

I stayed ten minutes longer than I should have, hemming and hawing in the kitchen, waiting for the sound of footsteps in his room.

They didn't come.

Why I was waiting? It was ridiculous. Stupid.

Why should I care about Cal Gatlin?

He meant nothing to me.

That's what I told myself over and over as I rode to school after a morning of stalling. And what I told myself at school, every time I walked through the halls, scanning them for signs of Cal. And what I told myself when I went home and he was nowhere in sight.

Even at home, Cal dodged me, remaining in his room unless absolutely necessary. Even then, he avoided eye contact as if we existed in entirely different realities. This went on for a week. Every day made me more and more anxious.

By Monday, I was going crazy.

I had to talk to him, even if it was ridiculous.

Jess met me in the hall on the way to lunch, chattering that Nate was off at a swim meet and something about Vanessa Miller convincing the other cheerleaders to go cheer them on. She steered clear of the topic of my new stepbrother.

I appreciated it.

And at least the whispers and looks at school had calmed. Now that it was clear I would (probably) not be murdered, I was no longer fun gossip material.

We made our way to our usual table—this time without Nate, which was good, because the first thing I did when I sat was scan the room for Cal. My eyes landed on him tucked away in a corner of the room, leaning against a barrier and gulping a bottle of (what I hoped was) water.

I stood.

"What are you doing?" Jess said in a hushed voice, as if just looking at Cal invoked bad mojo.

"I don't know," I admitted as I crossed the room to him.

His head turned to watch me.

A knowing smirk lit up his face. He had had his eye on me the whole time, and we both knew it. It made my stomach turn, but I wasn't about to chicken out now.

His eyes followed me as I met him at his hiding place.

"Morning," he said.

"So are you going to come sit down or what?" I asked, crossing my arms self-consciously.

He raised an eyebrow. "Is this an invitation?"

I didn't answer, just waited. His full lips curved into a smile. My heart jumped and quivered in response.

No, stop feeling like that.

"Change of heart since the last time?" he asked, cocking his head to the side.

"Yeah. Well. We're family. So."

"Not afraid your boyfriend will get his ass beat?"

"Nate isn't here."

I cringed at the way his smile grew, realizing what an

utter cop out of an answer that was.

"Oh, yes," I added in a sharp voice, "of course Nate would get his ass beat, that's why I've planned it all out like this. You got me. I would have gotten away with it too, if it wasn't for you kids and that pesky dog."

"Hm. Having strange men over while the hubby's away. Kinky."

I rolled my eyes at him, ignoring the way my body reacted to his voice saying kinky.

"Are you coming or not?"

To my suprise (and, strangely, excitement) he didn't tell me to fuck off or keep teasing me. He slid his hands into his leather jacket and strolled toward the table where Jess was shaking like a spooked rabbit. I took a deep breath as I followed him. This was a terrible decision.

But then again, most of my decisions were.

"Morning to you too," he greeted Jess. She sat there with wide eyes, staring at him like he might stab her at any moment. Which, granted, was a possibility, given the rumors that surrounded him. He stuffed the water bottle into his jacket.

Despite myself, I rolled my eyes again. But not at Cal. At Jess this time. I took me aback that I was defending Cal like that, even if only in a small way. But it was true. He was an asshole, but he wasn't that bad.

Oh my God, can you hear me?

Cal Gatlin? Not that bad?

What was this boy doing to me?

"Jess, this is my, uh… my brother," I said, by way of an awkward introduction.

She nodded shortly. I could practically hear her heart hammering in her chest. Mine was the same.

"Stepbrother," he murmured, leaning back in his chair. His cool gaze landed on me and lingered for a moment too long.

"Yeah. That."

Cal sized up Jess as I picked through my salad, wondering why in the world I did this in the first place. I had a million things I wanted to ask him. And a few things to interrogate him with. Namely how he could go from so hot to so cold. From the downright nasty man who had asked me to say cock for him to the gentle one that had tended to my bruise.

I sorted out my thoughts, preparing to start in on the Spanish Inquisition, but I didn't get the chance. Because Jess had built her courage up first, and her head peeked up to stare at Cal again.

"If you're here to kill Nate," she said, "he's gone."

"Really? Damn." Cal cracked his knuckles. "Guess I'll have to stick around until he comes back."

A few freshmen at the table next to us glanced over and whispered with wide eyes and gasps amongst themselves.

Jess frowned.

"It's not funny, you know. Causing shit for Natalie.

She has it hard enough as it is." Her eyes were still wide and terrified, but her chin tipped up defiantly.

Wow. Go Jess. She cared about me, of course— she was my best friend. But I didn't think she'd go so far as to put her life on the line by sassing Callum Gatlin. Cal didn't seem to expect it either, and his impressed smile appeared, the one he saved for whenever I told him to fuck off.

"I ain't here to hurt anybody. Least of all Nat."

Nat. My nickname rolled so easily off of his tongue.

Jess noticed too and glanced at me, incredulous.

"Are you even still with him?" Cal asked, turning his head. "He hasn't talked to you since last week."

I stabbed my salad, wondering how Cal would have known something like that. Maybe he was keeping better tabs on me than I thought he was. "I don't know. It's not like we were ever really, properly dating. We didn't even go to prom together last year."

"You get why that is, don't you?" he asked. "It's cause I called him out. Now he's scared shitless."

"Drop it."

"He never appreciated you anyway," Cal growled. "Pathetic that he's too fucking stupid—and too busy fucking other chicks—to see what he's got at home."

"What?"

The world froze around me.

"I said he's an idiot. Not like that's news."

"No. What did you say about … about other

chicks?"

Cal crossed his arms and leaned back, his gaze even.

"Don't tell me you don't know. You have to have known."

"That's ridiculous. I mean—yeah, we weren't really, properly dating, I guess, but we still...." I turned to Jess. "Nate would never...?"

Jess's expression made me want to vomit.

"Natalie," she said. She licked her lips, pausing to gather her thoughts. "I thought you knew. I mean, with Vanessa always around, and...."

She bit her lip, looking into my eyes. It was the same incredulous look that Cal was giving me. The pitying look.

"That's such bullshit," I said weakly to Jess. "Do you hear him? Bullshit."

Jess didn't answer, picking at the crust of her sandwich nervously, her gaze fixed on the table. My mouth went dry.

It was bullshit, wasn't it? Nate had his problems, sure, but he had never fucked around on me. I mean ... surely he didn't even have time for that between swim practice and studying and whatever else he did ... right?

I looked back at Cal, expecting to see his mocking gaze back. Instead he was just sad.

"You really don't know?"

"Fuck off, Gatlin."

"I'm not antagonizing you. I told you, I'm sorry I

was an asshole earlier. But I'm telling the truth now."

Jess's head lifted, and she sucked her bottom lip as she watched us. I could read her expression: Cal Gatlin told someone he was sorry? That was the biggest bullshit of it all.

But it was true. And if that was true, what else could be?

Oh God. I was going to be sick.

"I've got to go," I said, stuffing my lunch back into my backpack. Where was I going? Why did I have to go? I didn't know. I just knew I was feeling dizzy, and the sound of Callum's words kept echoing in my head: fucking other chicks, fucking other chicks, fucking other chicks.

My stomach twisted again.

I had to get to a bathroom before I vomited.

"Natalie, wait—" Cal said, standing up with me. His voice was soft. It was warm and comforting instead of the hard orders that Nate would give. He reached out a hand to me.

I flinched.

His eyes went dark, and his jaw locked. His anger wasn't directed at me, but it didn't matter.

"I have to," I choked, shaking my head and stumbling. "I'm sorry. I can't."

CHAPTER 7

"Nat, can I come in?"

Cal's voice was joined by three sharp raps on my bedroom door. My eyes burned, and my cheeks were sticky with dried tears. A teardrop splashed against the glowing screen of my phone as I glared at it, my ass planted on the floor in front of my bed, silently begging Nate to text back.

I had been waiting for five hours with no response.

A bundle of missed calls from Jess flashed across the screen, but I wasn't ready to talk to her yet. I loved her, but I needed to talk to someone else. Someone who understood.

I wet my lips and rasped, "Come in, Cal."

Why did I let him in? I don't know.

I just knew that I needed him there with me.

Cal pushed the door open quietly and crept in, his expression solemn. He bit his thick lower lip as he examined me, and I saw that look his in his eyes again. But it wasn't pity, like it had been in Jess's eyes. It was empathy.

Cal hurt for me.

"Should I go?" he asked.

His flat voice hid the pain underneath.

"No." I shook my head. I refused to cry. And besides, the shock was numbing me to normal emotions.

Cal closed the door behind him and hesitantly walked towards me, taking a seat beside me on the floor. The warmth of his body wrapped around mine, melting the coldness that froze me. In my shell-shocked haze, I couldn't resist. I leaned over and rested my head on his shoulder.

He paused, confused. But after a moment, he melted into me, taking me into his arms like it was the most natural thing in the world.

"I can't believe it," I said. "I never thought…."

"I told you. He's a fucking idiot." Cal drew his arm around me tighter. I closed my eyes, enjoying the sensation. It was the first real warmth I had felt in a long time. "Has he admitted it yet, or is he too much of a fucking coward?"

I glanced at my blank phone, and he did too. "He might just have his phone on silent…."

Even I knew that was bullshit. Cal groaned.

"I'm sorry. If you'd let me, I'd kill him for you."

I rolled my eyes despite myself and gulped a laugh, shocked by how something so lighthearted could happen when I was so out of it.

"Vanessa Miller, though? And … and other girls?" I looked down at the hands in my lap. Callum's hands laced their fingers in mine. A strangely comforting movement. "I can't believe it."

"Yeah, well. He's a dick. I assumed you knew about it."

I nodded to myself even though I still couldn't process it.

I think I was nodding about something else—Callum being near me. Cal was so warm, so strong, so safe. I never wanted him to let go. His fingers began combing through my hair and he muttered soft, comforting words into my ear. His breath against my skin felt delicious.

I wanted to taste it.

I wanted to take Callum in and embrace him so hard that he became a part of me. It was stupid. But it was true. Even Mom, with her home grown Oprah wisdom, had never known me like Callum knew me, at least at this moment.

I remembered what he said the other day:

I see you. I know.

Still shell-shocked and a little out of my mind, I nuzzled my nose into his neck, inhaling the deep, masculine scent he had left on my pillow that night. Callum froze.

"Natalie?"

We met eyes for the first time since he sat down.

His gaze lowered, fixing itself on my lower lip and the way it opened and quivered for him. His tongue ran along his own lips as he watched me, and the pulse in his throat throbbed hard. His fingers pressed into my skin, drinking in the feel of me underneath his strong grip.

Something glowed behind his eyes, something hard and hungry and fiery. It had started warm, but now it was burning. It was something that made my stomach do little flips and my hands tremble.

Callum Gatlin wants me.

No. Impossible. Ridiculous.

But then why was he looking at me like that?

And why was his grip on me tightening? Not in the threatening way that Nate's did. In a new, strange way. One that made my trembling hands want to run their fingers through his dark hair.

No! He was my stepbrother.

Like I said, impossible.

The shock was tricking me. I was out of my mind. I was hungry for his warmth and concern and reading too much into it because I was desperate for someone. I should be ashamed.

"I should go to sleep," I said, closing my eyes and forcing the words out. I hated to say them. I didn't want him to go. But I had to get him out of here before I did something stupid.

"Are you sure?"

Cal's voice was strained. He didn't want to leave either. But I couldn't think about it. I couldn't do anything I would regret later. I shook my head, taking every last bit of will to force myself to give in to reason.

I was weak right now, and I was fucked up. I couldn't let my weakness fuck up another person too.

"I'm sure," I whispered.

CHAPTER 8

The rest of the week was hell.

Nate avoided me, disappearing at lunch and refusing to pick up his phone. Jess stayed with me. She explained that she have told me before had she known I was unaware about Nate cheating, and she dutifully handed me tissues under the bathroom stall door whenever I needed to cry alone.

It killed me to find out about all the girls Nate had ploughed through, and it killed me even more to know that he was too much of a coward to admit it to my face. But as the week went on and the initial shock wore off, I nursed a deeper wound:

The problem of Callum.

My cheeks burned with embarrassment every time I saw him, humiliated by my actions that night. I couldn't help but remember the way I had felt in his arms, the way I nuzzled his neck, the way his lip looked so bite-able. Or that I had let him see me cry and even let him stroke my hair. How could I be so stupid? So hormonal? So imperfect?

Callum Gatlin was beginning to captivate me. He made my act break down, and that terrified me. For the first time in forever, someone was opening me up, seeing me for what I really was.

I hated it.

By the Friday of that week, I had mostly cleaned up. Or at least I was sure I could go out wearing mascara and not cry it off. But I still I needed a plan. I couldn't let Nate win like this. I couldn't let him have the satisfaction of seeing how badly I was taking this whole thing.

And most of all, I needed to get out of the house, because being alone in a bedroom with Cal Gatlin and his strong arms and his delicious scent was the last thing I needed.

I slapped on some lipstick and called Jess.

"Do you need ice cream?" she said, answering the phone on the first ring. "I can be over with some Ben and Jerry's in, like, ten minutes."

I smiled. "No. We're going to the football game."

I could sense her smiling back at me on the other side of the line. "Thank God," she mumbled. "I thought you were dying."

Close, but I wouldn't give Nate that, either. Sobbing pathetic Nat was gone. Here comes vengeful bitch Nat.

"You know he's going to be there, right?" she asked, as if she could read my mind. Then again, we were best friends—she probably could. "Nate, I mean. Are you sure you want to go with him there? I, uh, I heard he was going with Vanessa...."

Shit. That stung.

"Good. I want him to fucking see me." I pulled my t-shirt off and sifted through my closet. This changed everything. This wasn't just some empowerment mission to make me feel like a functioning member of society—now I was angry. "I'm wearing Maneater, then."

Jess laughed. "God, Maneater? To a football game?"

"Desperate times call for desperate measures."

"True." She snorted a laugh again, and I heard the jingle of her car keys. "I'll be over in ten. Wear a push-up bra too, he'll hate that."

I ended the call and threw my phone on the bed. The sky was turning golden with the sunset, which meant I had about thirty minutes to pull on something sexy and get down to the field before the game started. My closet wasn't cooperating, and I dug through it harder, searching for the blood red silk I needed. I had almost forgotten I was half naked when I heard the creak of the door being pushed open.

I turned around, expecting to see Mom, but froze when I realized who it really was.

Callum.

"Sis, you got any—"

He froze in the doorway, and his eyes grew wide. My mouth went dry when I saw his gaze lower, falling on my chest. My breasts were just barely covered by the black lace of my bra, now rising and falling with my panicked breaths.

The cold air of the room gave me goosebumps as it carressed my soft, exposed flesh—or was that Cal's gaze I was feeling? Mom hadn't given me many of her curves, but what she did give me in the chest department was nice. Callum apparently thought so too, because he opened his mouth as if to speak, but was speechless.

He licked his lips, trying to find something to say.

"Cal," I rasped. "You should have knocked—"

"Shit, sorry!" He shook his head, snapping out of it. Crimson ran to his cheeks. "Jesus, Nat, I'm sorry. I should have—I should have, uh, knocked…."

He wants you, the annoying voice in my head whispered.

Shut up, I snapped back. Why was I so angry at the voice? Was I worried it was true?

I crossed my arms over my chest and watched as Cal turned away, his neck blushing red. He reached up and rubbed the back of his neck, obviously embarrassed as hell. Cal Gatlin? Being ashamed of something? I couldn't help but smile. It was strange, feeling that comfortable with him that I could smile at something so awkward. But it was real. It felt safe.

"You want something?" I asked. "Other than a peep show?"

Cal gawked. I did too. Did that really just come out of my mouth? Bitch Nat was a bold woman. I liked her.

"I—I don't remember," he stammered. His eyes darted to the door, looking for an escape route. I really was making him nervous. My smile grew. Adorable.

"I mean if you wanted to look at my boobs, you could have just asked."

He rolled his eyes.

"Look, do you have anything to say?" I asked. I glanced at the setting sun outside my window. "Because it's getting late, and I have somewhere to be."

"Where?"

"Football game. I'm goddam full of school spirit."

He snorted. "You know that douche will be there, don't you?"

"Jesus, does everybody in this town know what he's

up to besides me?" I snapped, throwing my hands up. My breasts bounced, and Cal's eyes glanced down again. Then away, his cheeks even redder. I was absolutely devastating this boy.

I wrapped my arms back over my chest again for his own protection. "Anyway, yeah, I'm still going. Deal with it."

"You can't," Cal growled. "Not while he's there."

"Don't fucking tell me what to do."

That was the one thing I had decided I was done with: stupid ass teenage boys deciding they get to control my life. Been there, done that, never doing it again. Even if this teenage boy in question happened to be wearing those thin sweatpants that revealed a little too much and made my mouth water.

"You sound like Nate," I added for good measure.

Cal winced. I hit him in a weak spot. Good.

"You know that's not what I meant. It's not safe."

"I like to live dangerously."

He rolled his eyes again, this time even more exaggeratedly. "If you're still going, I'm coming with you."

"Like hell you are. The last thing I need is another fight."

"You can't go out alone with him there, Nat. It's dangerous."

"I won't be alone. Jess is coming with me."

"Because she was so great at helping you avoid his

dickishness before."

"Don't talk about Jess that way."

"Sorry." He frowned. "But it doesn't change things. I'm coming, whether you like it or not."

I groaned. God, he was persistent. And I could tell I wasn't about to win this one. As distracted as he was by my still exposed breasts, Cal could be a stubborn ass when he wanted to be. And with the sun setting so fast outside my window, I had no time to waste in trying in to convince him.

"Jesus. Fine." I turned back to my closet and resumed digging. "Make sure you wear something decent, otherwise Furst will follow us all night."

"Yes, ma'am." The way he said ma'am made my heart flutter. "Do you need to hire me a babysitter, too?"

"Oh, fuck off."

He chuckled, and the dark, sweet sound did something to me deep inside. I squashed the feeling down, desperately trying to ignore it and focus on the search for Maneater as his footsteps padded out the door. They paused.

"And Nat?" his voice called.

"What?"

Cal leaned in the room again, this time all traces of shame gone from his face. He was back to being Cal Gatlin, the asshole, though maybe not as bad of an asshole as I had taken him to be. His gaze slithered down my body one more time, this time slow and sensually. A shiver trembled through my spine.

His gaze reached my eyes again, and there was that look in his face, the hungry one. Like he wanted to grab me, drag me to his bedroom by the hair, and just ravage me.

His cocky smirk played across his face.

"Thanks for the peep show."

CHAPTER 9

I found Maneater at the back of the closet, wedged between a prom dress and a swimsuit.

I pulled her out with a shit-eating grin.

Oh, yes, Nate would really hate this, I decided, modeling her in front of my mirror. She was my one and only sexy dress—not because I objected to sexy dresses, but because she was perfect. No other dress could beat her.

Maneater was a sinful red color with a plunging neckline and a slit that revealed a strip of leg up to the thigh. It stretched over my body perfectly, highlighting every little turn and curve in the most flattering way possible. Not anywhere near what somebody should wear to a Friday football game, which was even more perfect.

Nate would know this was for him, and he'd know he'd never get to touch it again. I practiced a few hair flips and some hip swaying in the mirror.

You go, Bitch Nat.

I grabbed my purse when the rumble of Jess's car roared up to the house, her headlights flooding my room through the window. Cal was leaning against the bannister of the stairs, waiting dutifully for me.

I gaped at him.

He cleaned up very, very nicely. A thin black t-shirt stretched tight over his muscles, and the leather jacket he had shrugged on gave him a badass look to match the motorcycle parked outside. His jeans were still dark and distressed, but at least they were clean. His perfectly messy dark hair was combed back from his face, giving me a full view of the dark five o'clock shadow and tattoos that licked his neck.

He glanced up at me, and his lips parted.

"Jesus, Sis," he breathed, dragging out the word Jesus as long as it took his gaze to roll down my body.

I smiled. I loved being a jaw-dropper. Especially if the jaw dropping belonged to Cal Gatlin.

No. Stop thinking like that.

"Hell, Sis," he choked. "Why don't you wear that around the house more often?"

"It's not for you," I said, tilting my chin up. My heartbeat was fluttering like a hummingbird's wing. It was true, it wasn't for him. So why did I want it to be for him so badly?

"Then....?" he asked, cocking an eyebrow.

"It's for... well, it's for Nate."

His expression turned dark.

"You're not going back to him, are you?"

"Fuck, no. I want him to stare at my ass and think about how he'll never get to touch it."

He threw his head back and laughed.

"I knew you weren't as good as you pretended to be, Sis. Now I have to go. Gotta see that douche's face."

I half expected him to throw his arm over my shoulders as we walked out, but chastised myself. I didn't know what had gotten into me, but I couldn't keep thinking of him like that. No matter how delicious he smelled. Or how strong his arms looked in that jacket. Or, God, how great his butt looked in those jeans.

Jess met us outside with a raised eyebrow.

"You two look awfully close," she said, barely withholding judgment. "Are you riding in my car too?"

"I've got a bike," Cal said, shaking his head. I had seen the motorcycle before, a glossy black monster that

Cal babied like his own infant.

We waited for him to mount and get the engine going. The purr of the bike, plus the sight of Cal working so expertly with it, did things to me. He glanced up and smirked at my expression.

"You want a ride too, Sis? Plenty of room for us to get up close and personal."

I scoffed, but Jess laughed.

"No, do it," she said. "Jesus, can you imagine Nate's face if he sees you riding up on that thing with your arms around Cal Gatlin?"

That ended that argument.

I hopped on faster than the Flash and wrapped my arms around Cal's chest, mounting the bike behind him. He helped me find my seat. His rough hands slid along my legs and grasped my thighs, pulling them apart to demonstrate how to sit behind him without falling off. I squeezed up against him as his strong hands held my body, fitting me into him like a puzzle piece. My chest pressed against his back, and my face was nuzzled in his neck again.

God, he smelled so good.

"I knew I'd get between your legs," he murmured in my ear, turning his head just enough that I could see the cocky smile.

I pinched his arm, attempting to scold him but shocked by how nice his warm muscle felt underneath my hand. He chuckled, and the sound reverberated through his chest under my grasp. It was almost as good as the vibration between my legs.

No, no, no, don't think about that! Especially not with Cal Gatlin!

I chased the thought of my mind as Jess left and we peeled out of the driveway behind her.

The game had already started by the time we arrived, so most people were distracted. I did catch a few double-takes as Cal pulled in on his bike with my arms wrapped around him.

Cal chuckled again. He was doing that a lot lately.

"You have admirers, Sis."

"More like rubberneckers. They're watching the train wreck."

"You think we're a train wreck?"

"No," I said too quickly. Though I had to admit. Even if this train was wrecking, I never wanted to get off.

Cal and I hopped off, and we followed Jess to her favorite spot to watch the game. I felt his warm hand rest at the small of my back as he led me to the bleachers. Electric sparks shocked my body wherever his skin met mine. I closed my eyes hard, praying he didn't notice.

Don't think about that, don't think about that, don't think about that.

"Ooh, hold on, I think I left my keys in the car," Jess said, slapping her forehead. "You two go sit down without me, I'll be right back."

"Is she really sure she wants to leave you alone with me?" Cal asked, leaning over to whisper in my ear. His warm breath rolled down my neck in a delicious way. Goosebumps rose on my skin. "Isn't she afraid for her friend, the good girl? Doesn't she know I'm bad? Everybody else here does."

I rolled my eyes, but when I glanced back at him, his gaze was lingering a little too long on my ass. I lost my breath for a moment. Not out of fear. Out of something I refused to admit.

"Gatlin, are you checking me out?" I squeaked.

"Can't blame me. Jesus, Sis, I can't believe you've had that dress hidden from me for so long."

"Please. I'm a dork. I'm not half as beautiful as those girls you're always chasing after school."

"I think you're incredibly beautiful." He thought about it for a moment, considering his next words. "And fucking sexy."

I shivered.

No, no, no. Stop!

"You don't have to spare my feelings, Gatlin. I'm fine being a dork."

Cal's brow furrowed. "I'm not sparing anything. Look over there."

I glanced over. A huddle of freshman boys that had been staring at us immediately turned red and looked away, muttering to themselves.

"So what?" I asked, irritated. "More freshmen gawking at the train wreck."

"It's not me they're looking at, Sis."

"What do you mean?"

He looked at me like I was a moron. "You have to know what you do to men. You have a dress called Maneater."

"It's a joke," I said in a small voice.

"Well, it ain't a joke that every boy in this school would do anything to get under that skirt." He crossed his arms and looked out into the game evenly. "They don't stare at us because we're a train wreck. They stare because they want you. And because they can't have you—because you're mine."

"Please. That's not even close to true."

You're mine, you're mine, you're mine.

Cal looked over at me, his eyes searching mine. "Whether you believe it or not, Sis, it's true. You're fucking beautiful."

I opened my mouth to say something back, but I couldn't think straight. Cal Gatlin thought I was beautiful.

My lower lip quivered for a moment as I wracked my brain for any coherent thought, and Cal's gaze floated downward and fixed on it. He reached forward and ran his thumb along my bottom lip, leaving me paralyzed.

"You know how many boys would do anything to

bite that lip?"

Cal Gatlin was touching me.

Holy shit.

But it didn't feel wrong like when Nate touched me. It felt safe. And it felt warm, and it felt... sexy. I wanted him.

Cal looked deeply into my eyes. His fingers caressed my jawline, and his lips parted.

This was it. I could feel it. I wanted to kiss him. I was going to kiss him. I was going to open myself up to Cal Gatlin and taste him.

Everything happened in slow motion: the electric touch of his fingers pulling my jaw towards him, the expectant opening of my mouth, the warmth of his breath rolling down my neck...

"Gatlin, what the fuck do you think you're doing to my girlfriend?"

The sound of Nate's voice broke us apart. Cal's hands dropped, more out of confusion than fear (as if Cal could ever be afraid of Nate). We turned.

Nate was marching down the sidewalk toward us, his shoulders thrown back and his glare mad as hell. I noticed Vanessa Miller waiting worriedly in the distance. She was wearing his varsity jacket. My stomach turned.

It was true, wasn't it? Nate really was fucking around on me with her. It was one thing to hear it, and it was another to believe it. But it was nothing compared to being faced with the evidence firsthand

and being forced to really feel it as the whole situation dawned on you.

I was going to be sick.

"Ain't doing anything to your girlfriend. She looks fine where she is." He nodded towards Vanessa. His voice was bored and flat, but I could feel his grip tightening on my hand. It wasn't a dangerous or painful one, like the grip Nate always had on me. It was protective.

"Fuck off, Gatlin, and get your hands off of her."

"Why? Afraid she's found someone who gives a shit about her? You're right."

Nate marched up to us, and Cal subtly pushed me behind him, shielding me with his chest. What was Nate thinking, getting in Cal's face like that? He was a moron, but not that stupid. Especially after what had happened earlier in the cafeteria. He had to know that there was no way he could beat Cal. So why was he provoking him so much?

"Please, don't," I said, touching his arm. Cal's arms dropped just as quickly as they had the first time. It felt strange, being listened to. It felt like I mattered.

Of course, like everything else in our relationship, Nate had to ruin that moment of peace too.

"Fuck off, Natalie," he spat.

"Don't fucking talk to her like that!"

Cal dove forward with a punch that connected with a sickening smack and landed Nate flat on his back.

"Cal!" I cried. Vanessa Miller was running forward now, too, and Jess was grabbing my arm to pull me back. Cal looked like he was intent on murdering him, and God, I couldn't have that. I couldn't have Cal be taken away from me like that. I couldn't let him do that to himself, not for my sake at least.

Nate was on the ground, struggling to pick himself up, and Cal lurched forward. Before he could beat the life out of him, I grabbed his arm again.

His hand grasp went limp, like he was afraid of hurting me. Another strange moment as the feeling of safety washed over me—it felt like I was worth not hurting.

"Please, Cal. Let's just go."

I suddenly hated Maneater and the dumbass revenge plot that made me wear her here. And I hated that I had seen Vanessa Miller wearing Nate's jacket, and I hated that I hated Vanessa Miller when I should feel sorry for her, and I hated that the people in the bleachers surrounding us were beginning to glance over and whisper to each other.

My grasp tightened on Cal's arm, and he groaned.

"Sorry, Nat," Cal growled. "I had to."

"No, you didn't."

His shoulders heaved, and his hands were still balled into fists. His veins popped against the muscles of his shoulders and neck, and it looked like it took every ounce of strength for him to not lurch forward again and murder Nate where he was still lying shell shocked on the sidewalk.

"You didn't fucking have to, and you know it. Jesus, Jess, go start the car. We have to get out of here."

"I'm sorry, Nat—"

"Don't. Let's just go. We have to get out before someone catches you."

I steered him away from the scene, praying to God that Furst was nowhere in sight. This was exactly the kind of thing he would love: an excuse to get Cal out of school and in a jail cell. And I wasn't stupid enough to think that Nate would forgive it out of the kindness of his heart, or even out of the fear of Cal coming back for revenge.

I kept a hold on Cal's strong arm as I pulled him away, back toward where we had parked the car and bike. He followed, keeping one hand on the small of my back. The scuffling of boots followed behind us, and Nate shouted out at us one last time:

"Where do you think you're going with my girlfriend, Gatlin?"

I whirled on him, finally pissed enough to bite back.

"I'm not your fucking girlfriend," I spat, grabbing Cal's arm as Jess steered us away. "And I never fucking will be again."

CHAPTER 10

The phone had been ringing all night. And now it was switched on silent and thrown under my bed, where I couldn't hear or see the dozens of missed calls piling up. The only sound in my bedroom was the soft creaking of the door as Cal crept in, and then the whisper of the sheet as he slipped into bed and wrapped his arms around me.

I rested my head on his shoulder. I was too worn out to fight the need to be with him. Besides—now that I was out of Maneater and into a camisole and pajama pants, there wasn't much sex appeal to worry about.

"I told you," he growled, his voice full of a repressed fury. "He's a fucking idiot. I should have beaten the moron out of him when I had the chance."

"Don't."

"I'm sorry, Nat." He nuzzled my face into his neck. "I wish I could fix it. I wish I could fix everything for you."

I did too. I pulled back to look at his face, still glistening with sweat from the near fight. I ran my thumb along the scar on his jaw, and his eyes closed.

"Are you alright?" I asked, tracing another scar. He had been in so many fights. I wondered if anyone had ever been this close to him without hitting him.

"I'm always alright when I'm with you, Nat."

I searched his face again. I didn't know what I was looking for, but I knew what I wanted. Because there, in my bedroom, alone at midnight with the moonlight pouring over his face, he had never looked so beautiful. The dark five o'clock shadow on his chin, the tattoos that laced across his collarbone, the deep color of his eyes burning like embers.

Maybe I missed Nate, maybe I needed someone to tell me they loved me, or maybe I just didn't know what else to do. But before I could think enough to stop it, I leaned forward, closing my eyes and opening my mouth for him.

He froze.

"Nat, what are you doing—"

"Do you want me?"

"I—" his voice choked again. "Natalie?"

There was a strange note in his voice. It was hesitant, but something was burning underneath it. He pulled away, but I grabbed his arms and held them where they were wrapped around me. He was ten times stronger than I would ever be, but he immediately relented, as if he could never resist me.

"Tell me. Do you want me? I have to know. It's killing me."

Cal swallowed hard. His lips and throat moving so intimately were mesmerizing.

"I want you so much it hurts me," he whispered.

"Then kiss me."

"Natalie," he breathed, his full lips parting just so slightly. I could taste his breath, pulling it into my own mouth with a sigh: the faint mint of toothpaste and the warmth of his throat. I could see his tongue move against his teeth just beyond the part of his lips, and the thickness of his bottom lip invited me to bite it. I wanted to. I wanted it in my mouth. I wanted him inside me.

"I shouldn't," he choked.

"You will," I answered.

I leaned up and caught his lower lip between my teeth. Something about that set him off. Before I could resist, I was on my back.

Cal's mouth fell on mine, hard and fast. No longer was this the soft, sentimental Cal that held me a few minutes ago. This was Cal on fire, desperate for me. His hands grabbed my waist, pulling me up against him so that nothing separated our bare skin. His lips brushed across my jaw, settling on my mouth and drawing the breath out of me with a kiss.

And it wasn't just a kiss. His arms crushed me to him, and his fingers dug into my thigh, taking handfuls of me wherever he could get them. His hips rocked against mine, hard, hungry, and insistent. I could feel myself growing wet, and almost as if Cal could smell the pheromones in the air, his kiss became more desperate. His fingers laced through my hair

I broke away from his mouth for a minute and moaned.

"Cal."

His body shuddered.

Then it froze. He broke away from the kiss.

"Oh, God," he whispered. His expression was horrified as he glanced down at our bodies, only the thin layer of clothing separating them. "Oh God, Nat, I'm sorry."

"Cal?"

He pulled away, panting. His eyes were wide. "I wasn't thinking. Jesus, Nat."

"Kiss me," I moaned, aching for the return of his weight on top of me. "I need you to kiss me again. Please."

"No."

"What?" I asked, breathless. I didn't have time to think. I needed more of him. I opened my mouth and leaned in again, desperate to taste him.

He pushed me away. "I said no. I can't."

I fell back onto my ass on the bed, my hands shaking. No? He didn't want me? Then why had he kissed me in the first place? I could feel the tears welling up again, despite all my will to crush them back.

"Then what the fuck was that?" I demanded. My voice was getting raspy with the pain. "Why did you kiss me? Was I just another conquest?"

Cal gaped at me. His expression grew furious.

"Jesus, Natalie, is that what you really think of me?"

"If I'm wrong, why won't you kiss me again?"

"Because…. Ugh." He shook his head and let it fall into his hands. "Jesus, Nat, you have no idea what you do to men. Of course I want you. Anyone with a working cock would want you."

My body reacted to the way the word cock passed his lips, and I ached to taste him again.

"Then why not?" I whispered, leaning forward to touch him. His hands shook as my fingers traced a tattoo on his bicep, and his eyes sank closed. He wants you, he wants you, he wants you, the voice said.

"Don't do that," he choked.

"What? This?" I continued to caress him, tilting my head and looking into his eyes, searching for an answer.

When his eyes opened, they were burning and hungry again. Before I could react, he grabbed my shoulders and pushed me on the bed. His knee pressed down between my legs, separating them, and his hands grabbed each ankle and pulled them around him. His intense gaze burned into my eyes as he grabbed my face and brought it to his, kissing me so passionately I couldn't breathe. My fingers raked through his hair, forcing his mouth to mine.

I gasped against him, parting my lips, and his tongue slipped into my mouth. His hips grinded against mine, and his fingers dug into my thigh. He pulled me so tightly against him that I could barely breath, and I loved it. The warmth of his skin on mine and the taste of his breath in my mouth made me starved for him.

He pulled away for a second, leaving me gasping underneath him. His gaze was on fire.

"This, Natalie," he growled, grabbing my hand and pushing it against the crotch of his jeans. I could feel his cock straining against them, hard and throbbing. I moaned, letting my eyes close, drinking in the sensation of it underneath my palm. Jesus, he was big. "This is what you do to me. Do you know how fucking much I want to tear off your panties and show you how much I want you? How much I need you?"

Unable to stop myself, I clasped my hand around his cock and felt it twitch underneath my fingers. He groaned a deep sound and buckled on top of me. His eyes rolled back into his head.

"Then do it," I breathed, digging my nails into the back of his neck, desperate to have his tongue in my mouth again. I didn't care if I was a virgin. I didn't care if he was my stepbrother. I didn't care if this was wrong. I needed him inside me. In more ways than one.

"Fuck, don't say that!" He pushed me away again, pulling himself up. His cock throbbed against the painful tightness of his jeans, and his chest rising and falling wildly. There was sweat on his brow, dampening his dark hair. His lower lip was swollen where I had bitten it. He had never looked sexier.

"Don't you want to fuck me?" I asked.

He looked into my eyes again, breathless, his chest rising and falling raggedly. "I want to fuck you so hard you forget your own name."

My fingers shook. I needed to wrap them around his cock again.

"Then why won't you kiss me?"

"Because it's wrong," he growled, sitting down with his head in his hands. His chest rose and fell harshly, still out of breath. "You're weak right now. You miss your boyfriend—as shitty as he is—and you've been crying, and then I come in and nearly fuck you, and it would be shitty of me to take advantage like that. I'm not going to use you."

"I don't fucking miss Nate."

"I still won't use you."

"Use me?"

Cal rested his head in his heads, his shoulders heaving as he caught his breath. "It's late. You're tired. I shouldn't be here."

Despite myself, I snorted a laugh through the tears. "You really are developing a moral compass, aren't you, Gatlin?"

He smirked. "What can I say, Nat. I'm a changed man." He stood. I could see the still see the huge bulge straining against his jeans, and the thought of what he might do with it once he got away from me and in private made my mouth water. His legs seemed shaky. "I need to go."

"Don't you want me?"

My voice sounded desperate, even to my ears. He paused, battling with himself.

"I will always want you, Natalie Harlow."

The words sunk into me as deeply as the rich, dark sound of his voice.

"Then I don't know why you won't stay."

"Because it's wrong, and I … I can't think straight. Not when you're looking like that, and moving like that, and moaning like that."

"What? Like this?"

It felt ridiculous, but I would do anything to keep him there. I tilted my head and let out the most orgasmic moan I could conjure, fluttering my eyes closed and letting my lips part. When I opened my eyes again, his whole body was shaking with the force it needed to stay where he was.

His jaw was twitching. His hands balled into fists.

"Yes," he choked. "Like—like that."

He stood in the middle of my bedroom, completely still except for his shaking hands. The fists had gone white, and it looked like his nails where biting into his skin. He couldn't tear his gaze from me. His jaw locked, and he forced himself to turn his head away.

"We can talk tomorrow," he said shortly.

He began making his way out of the room again.

"I don't know why you're suddenly such a gentleman," I said, desperate to keep him in my bedroom as long as possible. His head turned, pausing on the way out the door. "You've tormented me my whole life. Why did you hate me for so long? Why change now? Tell me that, Gatlin. If this wasn't just a conquest thing, then why have you hated me for so long?"

"I never hated you," he said gruffly, his eyes downcast.

"Bullshit. Then why did you harass me for so long?"

"Natalie," he said weakly. "Please."

"You were obsessed with me, with making my life hell. And now you want to fuck me? Why, Gatlin?"

"Quit pretending like you don't know."

"I don't."

He looked at me strangely. "You really ... you really don't know why?"

"If I did, I wouldn't be asking."

He looked at me evenly for a few moments, his expression unreadable. He opened the door and answered on the way out.

"Because I've always been in love with you," he said. "And I always will be."

CHAPTER 11

I couldn't sleep. I spent the whole night tossing and turning, trying to push the events of that night out of my bed.

But it was impossible. The sight of Cal's muscles glistening with sweat as he punched Nate, the taste of his tongue in my mouth, the feel of his hard cock against me as he pushed me down on the bed.... It was all too much. But what really stayed with me was the memory his deep voice.

"I will always want you, Natalie Harlow."

Ugh. It was too much for one night. I pulled a pillow over my face and managed to force myself to sleep.

Until I was woken by the sounds of banging in the kitchen.

My eyes fluttered open, pushing past the aching headache and the tiredness that sagged my eyes. I thought Mom would be at work that morning, but maybe I was wrong. I wrapped a robe around me and stumbled down the stairs, rubbing the sleep out of my eyes.

They widened when I entered the kitchen.

Oh Jesus. Not Mom. Cal.

And he was wearing ...

An apron?

"Morning, Nat," he murmured from his place at the stove. A wave of delicious scents hit me, and I realized the table was set with all sorts of food. Eggs and bacon, a tall pitcher of orange juice, and even a steaming kettle of tea. Cal glanced over and nodded at the table, motioning for me to sit.

Was it for me?

Cal the Romantic.

I guess there really is a first time for everything.

"You cook?" I asked as I took a seat. "Didn't know you had it in you."

"There's a lot you don't know about me."

"Sure thing, Martha Stewart."

He rolled his eyes, and a smile crept across his face. God, I loved seeing him smile. I watched the tattoos move with his muscles as he wiped down the counter, taking in how absolutely gorgeous he was.

Which reminded me. I picked up a spoon and shined it with my shirt until it was reflective, then grimaced.

"Gross," I said, examining my reflection in the spoon. "I look terrible. I am so not a morning person."

"Oh please," Cal grunted. "I told you. You're fucking beautiful."

My heart fluttered. I ignored it and stirred my tea, hoping he didn't realize how much it affected me to hear him say something like that.

"Are we going to talk about last night?" I asked finally, keeping my gaze fixed on the swirling tea. I couldn't tell if I wanted to or not. It would be humiliating, admitting that Cal made me so desperate for him. But I couldn't ignore it, not after he had me on my back with my legs spread. I was pretty sure that was the point of no return.

"What do you want to do?" he said, placing a plate of toast down on the table and taking a seat. "Talk or eat?"

"Both." I grabbed the toast, inhaling the delicious smell of crisp bread and warm butter. God, I loved a man who could cook. "You do the talking, I'll do the eating."

"Yes, ma'am." There was that playful glint in his eyes again. Jesus, didn't he know what that did to me? Probably—that's why he did it so much.

"You said you loved me. Bullshit or not?"

He dropped the asshole act in an instant.

"Never bullshit. Not with you."

"So you … you meant it?"

"Always."

There was a moment of silence as I contemplated that, running a finger along the rim of the teacup.

"So it wasn't…." I swallowed against the lump in my throat. "It wasn't just you trying to get into my pants, then? You meant it?"

His jaw dropped.

"You thought I was lying so I could fuck you?"

"Well, it was sudden, and you've acted like such an asshole to me before, and—"

"Natalie, I know you think I'm a fuckup, but I'm not that fucked up."

My face burned red. "I'm sorry."

He sighed. "It's not your fault. I don't blame you for thinking the worst of me, not after you had to put up with … that kid."

"Nate?"

His jaw locked, and he nodded shortly.

I looked down at my tea again.

"I didn't think anybody knew, you know," I said, frowning. "I thought I hid the bruises well enough."

"Not from me, Nat. I know you. Even if you don't want to be known."

I could stop my lip from trembling. It was a miracle he hadn't run screaming if he really knew me. I was the fucked up one here.

"And that's why you hit Nate?"

He grinned.

"It did feel good to hit the bastard. Wasn't all altruistic."

"And you'll never fucking do it again."

"Still have feelings for him?"

"No. God, no. But you can't get in trouble. Furst wants your ass in prison, and you know it."

"You going soft on me, Harlow?"

I smiled into my tea. "If you've appointed yourself as my personal bodyguard, I'm sure I'm fine. You're annoying as hell, but having you around has its perks."

He snorted, slipping his hand over mine and interlocking our fingers. It was such a simple motion, but it felt like Heaven.

"You have to promise you won't do it again," I said. "I mean it. I can't have you in prison. No more attempted murders, no matter how much he deserves it."

Cal rolled his eyes, that long, exaggerated motion that made him almost as sassy as Jess. But then he nodded.

"Thank you," I breathed in relief.

His cocky smile came back.

"So what do I get in return?"

"In … return?"

"Mm hmm." Cal leaned forward, and once again he was the seductive Casanova he had been last night. His hooded eyes gazed into me. "I made you a promise, so what are you going to give me in return?"

"I … um…." My throat was dry. My mother had given me a lot of home grown wisdom, but none of it covered when your dead sexy criminal stepbrother wanted to bang you on the kitchen table. "What do you want from me?"

Cal smiled.

Oh God, I shouldn't have asked that.

But instead of what I was expecting ("My face between your legs" or possibly "Your ankles on my shoulders"), he said:

"Can I kiss you again, Nat?"

He glanced down at my trembling lip.

"God, I love your mouth." His thumb ran along my lower lip. "Do you know how much I've dreamed about biting that?"

I swallowed hard. "What if someone catches us?"

He smile crookedly, then leaned forward, brushing his lips against my ear. "They won't," he whispered. "I told you, Nat. I'm good at being bad. I never get caught." He kissed my jaw. "Would you like me to show you how bad I can be?"

God, yes.

"Hm. Didn't think you'd be that enthusiastic."

"Shit, did I say that out loud?"

He chuckled and ran his lips across my throat. I couldn't stand it anymore. I needed him.

"Yes. Okay," I said. "Kiss me."

"You have such a way with words, Pink."

"Don't call me th—"

Before I could finish, his lips were on mine, warm and soft and sweet. A soft moan escaped my mouth. God, he tasted amazing. He tilted his head a little, opening his mouth, and I eagerly answered the movement with my own. Our lips fitted together so perfectly, like two pieces of the same puzzle.

The sharp squeal of a car skidding along our road snapped me out of my Cal induced trance. I froze.

"Shit!" I breathed.

God, what if it was Mom, or James? And they walked into me kissing my stepbrother at the kitchen table? I pulled away immediately, slapping a hand over my mouth and looking at the front door in horror.

Cal just snorted.

"Don't worry. They're gone," he said, reading my mind. "We have the house to ourselves for the whole day."

"Oh." I let my hand down. Cal's hand slipped over it again, comforting and gentle.

"If it makes you feel safer, we can go to my room."

"Now I know you're trying to fuck me."

Cal grinned. "Can't blame me, can you?"

His gaze lowered to linger on my chest seductively, and my heart stopped again. God, I loved when he looked at me like that. His fingers traced my palm, and he growled a sigh.

"You really are gorgeous, Nat. That isn't bullshit either, whether you believe it or not. Do you know how much I've wanted to suck on those sweet t—"

The sound of an engine roared outside the door. My grip on his hand tightened.

"Nat, we're fine. I told you no one's coming home."

"I hope so, if all you're after is sucking on my tits."

His touch disappeared, and I ached for it to come back.

"You know that's not what I meant."

"No, I believe you." I shook my head, trying to gather my thoughts. "I know you're teasing, it's just … this is all so fast. And I'm nervous. But I still want you. But I'm afraid." I groaned and put my head in my hands. "I don't know what I want."

Cal's hand slipped over mine again.

"I told you, Nat," he said in a soft voice. "I don't want to use you. I care about you. And I'll take whatever part of you you're ready to give me." His thumb rolled calming circles into my palm. "I don't deserve you, Natalie Harlow. I want you—God, I want you so fucking bad—but I'm ready to wait. And I can wait a long time. I'm stubborn as shit."

"You are a stubborn ass," I agreed.

"Thank you, sweetheart."

God, it was amazing to hear him call me sweetheart. But then another car screeched outside our door. I flinched.

Cal rolled his eyes. "Come on, let's go before another car comes by. We can't have a conversation with you freaking out every two seconds."

It was true. And the curiosity was burning inside me.

I had no idea what Cal's room looked like, I realized. The boy had lived in my house for nearly two months by now, and I had never even wondered what it looked like inside the mancave he retired to every evening. And the thought of being alone, in privacy, with him was almost too delicious to bear.

"Alright," I said, standing and letting him lead me up the stairs.

Time to bravely go where no woman had gone before.

Bella Scully

CHAPTER 12

Cal's room was mind-blowing.

Not because it was a terrifying jail cell or a dungeon or anything else I had imagined in my nightmares ... but because it was normal. Too normal for Cal. I sat on the gingham bedspread, glancing over the bare white walls and the single backpack slung on the floor. He hadn't bothered to put any decoration up, and the room felt hollow with only a bed, desk, and small wardrobe.

Cal leaned against the doorframe as he watched me examine his room. His even gaze was fixed on my face again, and I realized he was waiting for a reaction.

"No decorations?" I asked, breaking the silence.

"I didn't expect to be staying here long."

"Really?"

"Our parents don't exactly get along, Nat."

"Wait, what?"

I was momentarily distracted from the confusing bedroom. I hadn't noticed anything wrong between Mom and James. Though then again, I was probably too busy trying to survive living with my terrifying stepbrother to notice anything outside of that goal.

"What do you mean?"

"They fight. All the time."

He cocked his head and took a seat beside me. His hand rested on my knee, and once again electric sparks flew out of it. "You really haven't noticed?"

"I guess I was distracted."

Cal's cocky grin reappeared. "By what?"

Shit, shit, shit, shouldn't have said that.

"By ... uh ... well, by you."

Shit! Really should not have said that.

Cal's hand slid a little up my thigh. My breath caught. God, that felt good.

"Really?"

"Yes."

"In what way?"

"In the I-don't-want-to-be-murdered-by-you way."

He laughed, not realizing how true that was, at least when it came to the first week we had lived together.

Relief flooded me when he didn't move his hand away. Having him so close to me, so intimately, was doing things to me. Not to mention that the warmth of his body was sinking into mine. I could feel his heavy form pressing against me—not dangerously or intrusively, but magnetically.

I wanted him closer.

"Are you sure that's it?"

"Well, there's also the I-want-him-inside-of-me way."

Shit, Nat, keep shoving that foot further down your throat.

But it was true, and I knew it. And I wouldn't take it back.

Cal's eyes grew wide, and his grip on my thigh unconsciously tightened a little.

"Jesus, Nat. Did that really just come out of your mouth? You really aren't as innocent as you pretend to be."

He made a move to get up, and I grabbed his hand. "No, don't go! I'm sorry, I wasn't thinking—"

He gave me a strange look. I realized his chest was rising and falling a little faster, and there was a blush crawling up his cheeks. He wasn't embarrassed—he was turned on.

"You didn't do anything wrong, Nat. It's not your fault."

"Then why are you leaving?"

"Because ... Jesus, Nat. Because if I don't, I'm going to do something really, really stupid."

"Like what?"

"There's a beautiful woman in my bed, we're home alone, and she just said she wants me inside her. Take a wild guess."

My heart raced. He motioned to move again, but I grabbed his arm and forced him back onto the bed.

"Why is that stupid? Do you ... do you not want me?"

His jaw dropped again, and I got that you-cannot-be-serious look. "Nat. How can you even ask that? I told you I—" He choked on his words a little, but then cleared his throat. "I told you how I felt about you. I will never not want you."

"Then why is it stupid?"

He groaned and let his head fall in his hands. "I told you, Nat. I'm bad for you. I'm not perfect like you are. You deserve so much better than me."

"Don't say that."

"It's true. And I told you. I'm not going to use you."

"What if I want you? Have you never thought of that?"

"You don't want me. I'm not your type, Nat. I'm an asshole."

"You said it before yourself. Good girls like me always want bad boys."

"I was just teasing you—"

"But it's true. I want you, Cal." I leaned forward and brushed his cheek with my lips. The rough stubble of his unshaven cheek scratched against my skin. He froze.

"Nat ... please don't say that if you don't mean it."

"I mean it. Kiss me."

His eyes searched mine for a moment, looking for permission. It was there. I wanted him.

I had always wanted him, I realized. Not the asshole him, the mask he hid behind. But the real him. Callum Gatlin, who punched my abusive boyfriend when I was too afraid to. Who held me when I cried. Who knew I hated him and protected me anyway.

I parted my lips, never breaking eye contact with him.

Helpless, he leaned forward, and his open mouth met mine. He tasted amazing. God, I wanted him.

"Fuck, Nat," he breathed.

His mouth pressed harder against mine, and his tongue slipped inside me. I moaned against his mouth, and that just made him more desperate. Before I knew what was happening, his arms had slipped around my waist and pushed me back onto the bed.

"Please," I whispered.

I was desperate for him. I didn't care it was wrong, I didn't care about anything anymore. All I cared about was how good Callum's strong hands were biting into my hips and how delicious his tongue was in my mouth.

"You have no fucking idea," he panted. His fingers ran through my hair, and I dug my nails into his back. "No fucking idea how long I've wanted to do this."

"Don't stop," I whimpered.

His hands groped their way down to my hips, looping the thumbs underneath the waist of my pajama pants. It happened so smoothly—like he had done this a million times before. Knowing Cal Gatlin's reputation, it probably had.

Oh God, I panicked as his fingers tugged my pants down. A moment of clarity hit me. I was going to be horrible at this. I was a virgin, and Cal Gatlin was Cal Gatlin. There was no way I could keep up with him.

Cal sensed my fear and stopped. One hand carressed my cheek. "Look at me, Nat."

Ugh. I hated to. The heat was already creeping into my cheeks. I was humiliated enough without looking like a tomato.

"Please," he whispered.

I met his eyes again.

God, he was beautiful.

"If you don't want this, Nat," he said, rubbing my cheekbone with his smooth thumb, "we don't have to."

"It's just—I've never—"

"I know."

Oh, hell. Was it that obvious?

He smiled at my expression, and I ducked my head. He kissed my forehead. "Natalie, I'm not going to fuck you, if that's what you're worried about."

"What?" I peeked up. "Then what are you doing?"

He gave me a wolfish smile that made my stomach flip.

"Just watch," he ordered.

Slowly, Cal's lips traveled down my cheek to my throat. His teeth nipped my earlobe on their way down, sending electric trembles down my body. Oh Jesus, that's good. His hands slipped down my waist back to my waistband, pulling my pajama pants down as his tongue dipped into my navel.

The cool air washed across my stomach as Cal's hand slipped between my legs. His fingertips traced their way down my inner thigh, feather-light and gorgeously warm. Cal's lips pressed against my hip, then down between my legs. He kissed the soft flesh of my thighs as he pried them apart.

"Are you alright, Nat?" he whispered. His warm breath rolled across the thin cotton of my panties.

"Yes," I moaned.

"Are you sure you want this?"

"Fuck yes!"

He chuckled deeply, and more of his warm breath licked against my thighs.

"Good girl. Now spread your legs."

"What are you going to—"

Cal's mouth nipped at my panties.

I gasped. God, god, god, that was good.

He chuckled again, pulling back to nip and kiss my inner thigh. The vibration of his voice between my legs was mind-numbingly wonderful.

"God, I love when you make that noise," he growled.

Cal's hands spread my legs, pulling me open for him. His lips pressed against my thigh again, grazing the skin as he took the thin cotton of my panties in his teeth. Slowly, he pulled them down with his mouth.

His lips traced down my leg as he undressed me. The warm cloth rolled down my skin, heated by his breath.

I felt the panties pulling off my foot, and Cal's head appeared back up between my legs. His cheeks were flushed, and eyes were dark and hungry. He carressed my cheek.

"Are you still okay, Nat?"

"Yes," I whispered, breathless.

His gaze slid down between my legs. I heard him suck his breath in, and his jaw began working. He licked his lips.

"Fuck, Nat," he breathed. His eyes were wide, and he rested his cheek against my thigh. "Your pussy is gorgeous."

Slowly, he leaned forward and kissed my clit.

I shuddered underneath him. Jesus, that was good.

He began tasting me in short, tiny licks, making my heart hammer against my chest. I had never known something could feel this good. I mean, I wasn't a complete prude—I had masturbated and fantasized before.

But now? With Callum Gatlin pulling my legs apart and laying the flat of his tongue against my pussy?

I was afraid I was going to explode.

Cal pressed his face into me and lapped hard. His tongue explored me, up and down and in little circles that left me gasping on the bed. His nails dug into my hips, forcing me against his face until there was no way for me to escape the pleasure. It built in me higher, tighter, and more painfully, pushing me to the edge.

My legs trembled around his head.

Cal's fingers locked in mine. "Tell me this feels good," he growled. He lapped against my clit, sucking hard.

"Y-yes," I gasped. "Oh God!"

"Put your fingers in my hair."

Shaking, my hands felt their way down to his face, brushing past the rough stubble along his cheek. I laced my fingers through his locks, pulling his face against me.

Cal growled in pleasure, purring amazing tingling vibrations against my clit that left me moaning and limp on the bed.

He sucked my clit hard, and there was nothing I could do to stop from screaming out in pleasure.

"Yes, Nat," he growled, holding my thighs down around his face. "Come on me. Come on my face, let me taste you. Fuck, you're beautiful."

I writhed against the bed as I came, digging my nails into his hair and moaning out his name. Cal, Cal, Cal. Gorgeous Cal, sexy Cal, bad boy Cal, Cal with his tongue up my pussy and his face covered in my wetness. God, he was good.

He kept lapping against me as I came, licking harder as my back arched and my eyes closed in ecstasy. So good. So, so, so good. Good didn't begin to describe it.

"Fuck, Natalie," he groaned against my pussy.

He waited until I collapsed on the bed, breathless and aching on the sheets. Then he pulled himself up to lay beside me, his mouth still glistening and his cheeks flushed.

"Kiss me," I whispered.

Slowly, he pressed his lips onto mine.

I could taste myself on him.

"Stay with me," he said, cupping my chin with a hand. I nodded, my mind already hazy with sleep. I doubted I could walk back to my bedroom after that anyway.

He kissed me again.

"Thank you, Natalie." Soft and tender, a tone I had never heard him use before. His arm slipped around me.

I fell asleep in Cal Gatlin's tattooed embrace, with his body cradling mine and his grizzled cheek nestled in my neck.

For the first time in a long time, I felt safe.

CHAPTER 13

I woke up to a hand clutching my mouth.

"Mmph!"

"Shh!" Cal pressed his lips against my ear. "Be quiet."

I tried to scream 'what the hell are you doing,' but it only came out as muffled growls. Cal's arms held me down in the bed, forcing me to stop my thrashing around. What the hell did he think he was doing?

I wondered if I should bite him. I was a good biter.

"Don't," he warned, watching me eye his hand. "Just wait, Nat. Listen."

"What's going on?" I demanded in a harsh whisper as he removed his hand from my mouth.

"I'm saving us."

"From what?"

"Do you trust me?" he asked

I considered that.

"Yes," I whispered back after a moment, sort of surprised. The whole time, I hadn't actually been afraid, just caught off guard. And not being afraid of Callum Gatlin? I was either crazy, stupid, or seeing a new side of him. Maybe all three.

He breathed a sigh of relief. "Then be quiet for just a few more minutes," he said into my ear. He nodded at the window. I peeked out for a moment and realized our parents' cars were back in the driveway.

"Shit," I whispered.

He nodded.

I know.

The fact that I was half naked in my stepbrother's room finally hit me. Even worse, half naked in my stepbrother's bed. Maybe we should have been more cautious about this.

Listening closer, I heard the sound of our parent's footsteps stomping around below us. I cocked my head at Cal. Stomping? My mom didn't stomp. If she did stomp, he must have really pissed her off. Cal petted my hair, burying his nose in my neck.

"What's going on?" I repeated.

"Just listen."

I heard muffled voices yell at each other, and my eyes widened again. Mom never yelled. Ever.

"Cal, tell me!" I whispered, eyes wide.

"They're fighting."

"I've never heard them fight before."

"Because you're always out, Nat," he said, rolling his eyes.

It was true. I guess I had forgotten just how much time I spent outside the house, dealing with school, extracurriculars, and my currently imploding relationships with my semi-boyfriend and increasingly distant best friend. "Do they really fight this much?" I whispered to him.

He nodded. His hand began stroking my hair. I realized it was shaking.

Cal Gatlin? Shaking?

Footsteps stomped up the stairs, and I heard James' voice yell something. I froze. Oh fuck no, he did not.

"Did he just call my mother a whore?" I demanded.

Cal's throat moved against my neck as he swallowed.

"I'm sorry, Nat." His voice was weak. It was the first time I had ever really seen Cal weak. There was fear in his voice.

"I'll kill him!"

I threw the blanket off, no longer caring about being found in my stepbrother's bed. All I could think about was Nate and James and how much I suddenly wanted to murder both of them. Cal's hand grabbed my shoulder and forced me back down on the bed. I thrashed against him.

"Let me go!" I yelled against the hand he clapped against my mouth. The footsteps outside our door in the hall paused.

"Nat, please," he whispered. "You've got to be quiet."

"He can't talk to my mother like that!"

"Natalie, please!"

His voice sounded truly pained now, but I didn't care. A switch had flipped in me after breaking up with Nate. I had had enough of men treating me and my mother like shit. And God help him if he thought I'd allow that in my own house.

But I didn't get the chance to rip his throat out like I wanted to. At that moment, the doorknob turned.

In a flash, Cal threw me sputtering under the covers. He launched himself up in one smooth movement, shielding the bed from sight. I peeked out of a small hole in the blanket, breathless and confused again. The door opened.

"Dad—" Cal started.

"Shut the fuck up."

James' voice was more venomous than I had ever heard before. Gone was the personable fifty-year-old with the desperate comb over and powder blue sweater.

The new James had enraged eyes and a sneer on his face. My stomach turned as I realized what it reminded me of—Nate when he dropped the mask he wore around other people.

"You think this is a fucking joke?" Cal's father asked him, taking a menacing step forward. "I heard you threatened another student at school again. We both know you're a fuckup, but I didn't think you were so fucking stupid to keep testing me like that!"

"Dad, it wasn't—"

"Shut the fuck up!" I heard a sickening slap as James' hand came down hard across Cal's face. Cal was sent stumbling back. He didn't fight back. He didn't even look up. Something about that made my heart twist hard.

James took another step forward. Instead of getting out of the way to avoid another blow, the smart thing to do, Cal moved in front of him again. Shielding me.

James' red eyes glared at him. Cal just kept his head down. Submissive. Letting it happen instead of fighting.

"You're just as fucking worthless as your bitch mother," James growled. Cal's hands clenched and unclenched into fists, but he didn't move. I put my hand over my mouth as James pulled his head back and spat in Cal's face. I wanted to scream at him, but I was paralyzed with fear. "You all are. Don't know why I ever fucking tried to deny that."

As suddenly as he had stomped in, James turned around. The door slammed behind him, leaving Cal frozen in the middle of the room. I was shaking, but I crawled out from under the covers. James could come back at any moment, but I didn't care. The look on Cal's face was breaking me.

"Cal?" I asked softly.

His head snapped up, like he had forgotten I was there. His expression softened. "I'm sorry, Nat," he breathed, walking to the bed and sitting down next to me. "I'm so fucking sorry you had to see that."

"Does it…" I touched the pulse that was racing in my throat as I tried to find the right words. "Does it happen often?"

"Yes."

"Why?"

I knew it was a stupid question, but I had no idea what to say. I was still in shock. I had never seen James like that.

Cal sneered. "Because I deserve it, didn't you hear?"

"You don't deserve it."

Cal nodded shortly. His thousand yard stare continued out the window into oblivion. When I touched his arm, he jumped, like for a moment he had been trying to forget he existed.

"But why does he do it?" I bit my lip, wondering if I shouldn't have asked that. It was a stupid question, and insensitive. He never asked me why Nate did it.

But he didn't seem to worried. He just sighed.

"Because my mom is dead. And I'm a fuckup."

"You're not—"

"Don't condescend to me."

I pulled back, afraid I was testing boundaries he didn't want tested. But I couldn't help it. "So he hits you because you have... problems?"

"And because I'm crazy," he added bitterly. "Haven't you heard? I'm a fuckup who needs attention, so I lie to people about my 'abusive' dad. Of course, James Gatlin could never abuse his son, he's too perfect, don't you know? It must be that his son is a liar. Must be that his son is a fuckup."

He swallowed hard.

"And if he can get back at me with his fists, well, all the better for perfect James Gatlin."

I didn't know what else to do, so I crawled to him again, putting a hand on his thigh. After a moment, he leaned into me and ran his hands through my hair. It was tender.

"I'm sorry you had to see that," he breathed. "And I'm sorry we're fucking up your family. I'm sorry he does that." He hung his head. "I'm sorry about everything, Nat."

"Did he ... did he do that to your mother as well?"

Cal's jaw locked. "Yes."

"I'm sorry too."

"Not your fault," he said in a small voice.

He kept his eyes fixed on the floor. I hated seeing him like this—crushed and small. I wanted the cocky Cal back, the one who called me Pink and begged me to say filthy things. More than that, I wanted the pained look to pass out of his eyes.

I wrapped my arms around him.

He jumped in his seat, his eyes widening as they glanced down at me snuggling into him. Then he melted in my arms, resting his head on top of mine where I had laid it against his chest. Cal Gatlin trusts me, I realized. Something shifted inside me, something secret and warm and shuddering in my heart.

"It's why I ... well, stalked you," he said after a moment. I snorted into his chest at stalked. The soft rumble of his bitter chuckle rolled against my cheek. His thumb began massaging small circles into my back. "The first time I saw that kid yell at you, I knew. The way you looked, Nat.... It was the same way my mother looked when he yelled at her. And I knew that I couldn't leave you alone. I already failed my mom, Nat. I couldn't fail you too."

"You don't have to save me."

"I'm not trying to save you, Nat." He kissed the top of my head, burying his face in my soft hair. "Not if you don't want to be saved. But maybe we can save each other."

"You think?"

"I think we already have."

He held me in the silence for a few minutes, my arms wrapped around his waist and his arms wrapped around me. His heartbeat drummed a soft thump against my ear. It was beautiful. It sounded like safety. It sounded like home.

"He hasn't hit my mom, has he?"

Cal's arms tightened around me. "No, Nat. Not yet. I won't let that happen."

I buried my face in his chest.

"I meant it when I said I love you, Natalie Harlow," he whispered, pressing his lips against my ear. "And I fucking swear, right here, right now. I will protect you. But only if you allow me to. I won't be here if you don't want me."

The tears had begun burning in my eyes, but even as choked up as I was, I knew what I had to say.

It rolled off my tongue before I could stop it:

"I will always want you, Cal Gatlin."

I kissed his neck, hoping it hid my blush. His arms tightened around me. He buried his face deeper in my hair.

"You have no idea how good that sounds coming from your lips, sweetheart."

Sweetheart.

Jesus, the boy was going to break me.

"You should go, Nat," he sighed. "Before Dad comes back. It's late, anyway. You should get back to your bedroom."

"No," I whispered, clutching at Cal's arm. He drew his embrace tighter around me. This was dangerous. I knew it. He knew it too. And yet absolutely nothing could make me leave him at that moment. I swallowed the lump in my throat.

Cal and I may be together now, I realized, but that didn't change anything. He was still my stepbrother, and he was still the bad boy with a bad reputation. We couldn't be together. If anybody found out, I knew it would tear us apart. Especially if it involved Cal Gatlin, the one everyone else had given up on.

But that didn't mean I had to.

I was ready to save him.

CHAPTER 14

The next day at school, my world was a blur. I wasn't sure what was going on as I floated through my classes, lunch, and after school meetings. All I could think about was James calling my mother a whore. All I could remember was the sickening sound of James' fist against Cal's cheek. All I could see was James and Nate and everything I've ever hated, their faces blending together until they were one monster that sunk its hooks into my brain and wouldn't let go.

But there was one candle in the darkness:

Cal is mine.

And I'm going to save him.

That one thought got me through the rest of the day, even as I constantly relived those horrible moments in Cal's bedroom. Did James suspect that I knew something? Why hadn't Mom told me he was like this? And why hadn't Cal ever told me before?

Because he thought you hated him, idiot.

Shut up, voice in my head.

I hate it when you're right.

The first I needed to do, I figured as I pulled on my backpack at the end of our afterschool prom committee meeting, was to figure out how to beak to Mom that James was a raging douche who needed to be evicted from the house. I mean, obviously she had to have known at least a little—he screamed at her.

But maybe she didn't understand just how bad it was, I thought as I pushed past the glass front doors of the school. Maybe I had to show her somehow. To save both her and Cal.

Maybe—

"Hey, Pink," a voice growled in my ear as I was locked in a strong embrace and lifted off the ground. My first instinct was to scream, but he knew me too well. A hand slapped over my mouth, stifling it before Furst could come running to save me from my murderer.

I bit down.

"Shit!"

Cal jumped back, grasping his bruised hand. I rolled my eyes as the drama queen inspected the light pink bite marks.

"I didn't even bite you that hard."

"Didn't your mother teach you not to bite your friends?"

My stomach turned a little as I remembered Mom and the situation with James. I pushed it out of my mind. That was a problem for another day. Specifically, another day where Cal wasn't getting grabby and assault-y again.

"Is there a reason you molested me?" I asked, placing a hand on my hip and pulling us into the alley behind the school. The last thing I needed was someone seeing his shenanigans and getting him arrested. "Or are you just trying to spice up our love life?"

Cal grinned and leaned forward, pressing his body against mine. "Hm. Do you think I should try?"

I pushed his grinning face away from mine as he tried to kiss me, unable to stop smiling myself.

"Stop. Someone will see us."

"Ooh, scandalous." He slipped an arm around me. "Incest is a good way to spice up the bedroom, yeah, Pink?"

"What are you doing, Cal?" I said dryly.

He pouted at my serious voice. God, he was cute.

"I wanted to ask you something, Pink," he said, rummaging around in his coat pocket. I eyed it suspiciously.

"If you're pulling out the condom, the answer is no."

"What's wrong, Sis, I thought you liked big cock."

I swatted him away while I blushed. "Not in public."

"That wasn't a no."

"I will murder you in your sleep."

He grinned and kissed my forehead. "Got it. Now pay attention, cause I've never done this before, and it's important."

"What is—oh no. No, no, no."

Cal dropped to one knee.

This is not happening.

"What are you doing?" I hissed at him.

"Proposing, dumbass."

"Cal, we are high school students!"

He rolled his eyes at me. "Yes, obviously, or there would be no point in me doing this. Jesus, Pink. For the smartest person I know, you can be pretty dumb."

"Nice backhanded compliment."

"No, it was a backhanded insult. I insulted you, but it was really a compliment. Pay attention."

I glared at him. He grinned up at me and leaned forward to kiss my stomach. Stop being cute, goddamnit.

"Alright. Fine. I'll play along." I pinched the bridge of my nose and took a deep breath. "Why wouldn't this work if we weren't high school students, Cal?"

"Because I'm asking you to prom."

"I—what?"

Now that was out of left field. For some reason, that struck me as even stranger than proposing marriage. Maybe because I had never associated something as innocent as prom proposals with someone as tattooed and foul mouthed as Cal. I eyed him even more suspiciously now as he pulled the mystery item out of his coat pocket, still not convinced it wasn't a condom.

No, I realized with surprise. It wasn't.

It was a small black jewelry box.

I really would have thought it was a wedding ring if he hadn't already nixed the idea. I tilted my head.

"Cal, I don't think this is how asking girls to prom normally works. You don't have to give me anything."

"Of course I don't have to. But I want to."

He flipped the box open.

I gasped as the glint of a diamond sparkled at my eye. It was the diamond stud that Cal normally wore in his ear. I hadn't even noticed it was missing. I looked into his eyes, even more confused now. I hadn't seen him take the earring off the entire time I had known him, now that I thought about it.

"Not ring," said Cal, holding it up for me. "I know you'd get pissed at that. But this is better. Like it, Pink?"

"Your … earring? You're giving me your earring?"

"Nope." He stood up, towering over me again. Delicately, he took my chin in his hand and tilted it up. His movements were so soft and careful, like he thought I was a china doll. He pulled the diamond stud out of the box and slipped into my left ear. He fastened it and pulled back again, tilting my chin to admire the way it sparkled next to my face.

"So…."

"It's not mine. It's my mother's earring."

"Oh."

I was frozen again. I didn't know how to handle emotional stuff like this, to be honest. I could ace the SAT, I could coordinate school club meetings, I could expertly avoid my abusive ex-boyfriend while maintaining perfect attendance in class. But I had the emotional intelligence of a potato.

"It's the only thing I have left of her," he said, looking into my eyes. "Dad took everything else. But these—" He reached forward to caress my jaw, dropping his fingertips over the diamond where it was secured in my earlobe. "I got these before he even knew they were missing. And kept them."

" 'These?' Is there another one?"

He nodded. His hand slipped into his pocket and pulled out the perfect twin to the earring in my earlobe. He placed the matching earring into his own ear. I loved the way it shined next to his eyes, bringing out their color and light.

Is that what Cal saw when he looked at me?

"There," he said in a soft voice. "Together again."

I stared into his eyes, mesmerized by how beautiful he was. And then caught myself, embarrassed, and looked down.

"You're so pretty when you blush, Pink," he said, cupping my chin again. He brought my face to his and kissed me long and deep. His tongue ran over my bottom lip. Not lecherously or lustily, but sweetly. I opened my mouth to him.

I loved him.

I loved him so fucking much.

"Why do you look so worried, sweetheart?" he whispered against my mouth. I tried to kiss him again, but he knew me, which meant he knew the whole 'emotional intelligence of a potato' thing. He avoided the kiss, waiting for me to answer instead of kissing away the question. I huffed.

"I'm worried about Mom."

"I told you I'd take care of you. That includes her."

"I know. But you're not always around. And I don't want to depend on you, Cal. I'm grateful, but I feel so useless. I want to be able to stand on my own two feet. I need to."

He touched my cheek. "We'll figure something out."

I closed my eyes. "You promise?"

"Always." He kissed me again. "Now come on, Prom Date."

"What—no!"

Before I could slap him away, he had grabbed me and slung me over his shoulder like a Viking claiming his war booty. Back to cocky Cal. Better than sad Cal, but still not great for me or my need to not be accosted constantly by an obsessed stepbrother. I went cross-eyed as his heavy footsteps bounced me up and down on his shoulder like a ragdoll.

"Put me down goddamnit!"

"Come on. I'll carry you in, princess."

"Oh my God. I'm really am going to murder you. I'm going to murder you in your sleep, and they'll put me in prison, and I'll graduate in a damp cell with my prison wife. You're so dead."

"Promise?" he asked, pulling me into his arms, cradling me like a baby. Less humiliating than over the shoulder, still not something I wanted my classmates to see. I glared at him.

"Yes."

"Thanks, sweetheart," he said with a kiss.

CHAPTER 15

The next few weeks were a rollercoaster.

One minute, I was glaring at Nate from across the lunch room—I had noticed he had started watching me again. The next, I was worried sick about the Mom and James situation, especially when the end of the semester approaching meant I was too busy to focus on it. And then there were all the little sweet moments in between with Cal.

Cal pulling me into a hidden part of the hallway for kisses at school. Cal slipping love notes under my bedroom door when the others were asleep. Cal giving me the eyes across the room when we were in public—a look that sent my heart racing and my cheeks blushing, which only encouraged him.

One night, Cal and I lay on his bed together, listening to Mom and James stomp around the lower floor. No screaming or fighting, but the stomping meant that something was up.

And, almost like he could read my mind, Cal had slipped into my bedroom and carried me out. Saving me from being alone. I fell asleep with his body curled over mine as we slept together in his bed, safe again. It was stupid. We could have gotten caught. It was dangerous and irresponsible.

So we did it every night for the next week. And then the week after that.

"Do you think they noticed last night?" I asked him one day as we walked into the lunch room. No more stares—people seemed to have gotten used to us being together. Hopefully as brother and sister. Though I suspected a few teachers were catching on, mainly because Cal had a habit of grabbing my butt when he thought no one was watching.

Cal snorted. "They don't notice anything besides themselves. Too self-absorbed."

"Don't talk about my mom that way."

He touched the small of my back lightly. A way of apologizing without saying anything too revealing out loud in front of the crowded lunch room. I appreciated it.

"She doesn't notice you, though," he said as we sat down.

I shrugged. "She's busy. She's a single mother. She doesn't have time to notice me. I'm fine with it."

"If you have to say you're fine so much, you're probably not. Quit trying to convince yourself."

I rolled my eyes. When I glanced back at him, he had leaned back in his chair and was watching my ear again. I felt the blush creep back into my cheeks. I loved the way he looked at me. Especially the soft look he got when he saw me wearing his earring, even if I had to hide it with my hair when we were at home. I doubted James cared about his son enough to notice the diamond stud, but I didn't want to risk anything.

"He's looking at you again," said Cal without removing his gaze from the sparkle in my ear. "No, don't look at him. Don't give him the satisfaction. But I thought you should know."

I grimaced and glared into my peanut butter and jelly. Jess plopped down in the seat next to me, but I didn't dare look up. Not now that I could feel Nate's hateful gaze on me again.

"Should I beat him?" Cal asked casually.

"Oh hush," Jess said, slapping his hand. Cal snorted, a smile perking up his face. Cal was warming up to Jess and her bold, brash, standing-up-to-tattooed-men-for-the-good-of-her-friend ways. "It's not like he's going to try anything."

"Don't tempt fate."

Cal frowned. "You should worry. I told you—"

"That he's dangerous but you'll protect me, yeah, yeah, I got it," I grumbled. Jess peeked up at us, interested. She knew something was up. But honestly, I didn't care anymore. All I cared about lately were the wonderful dreams I kept having in which Nate was tossed off cliffs or hit by busses.

"Do you want me to protect you now?" Cal asked.

His voice had changed. There was an edge to it, and he was sitting up in his seat. I felt, through the rising hair on the back of my neck, Nate's presence pass by me. I locked my jaw as I watched him walk away, gliding out of the cafeteria.

"You can protect me by sitting the hell down."

He gave a dramatic sigh, but relaxed now that the danger had passed. "Fine, Pink. But I'm worried about you. This doesn't feel right."

"You're imagining things," I said, ignoring the shaking in my voice. Jess's silent frown didn't agree with me.

I looked down at my lunch and repeated myself one more time, ignoring the echo of Cal's 'if you have to say you're fine so much, you're probably not' in my ears:

"It's nothing."

***

"Honey, have you seen Callum?"

I jumped in surprise, dropping my backpack on the kitchen floor with my hand still clenched around the doorknob. I glanced at the microwave clock: 6pm, the time I normally got home unless the student council meeting ran long. Mom knew that too, but she had never been waiting for me at home like this. Mom also hadn't talked me at all in about a week, I realized. Something about that made me sick to my stomach.

"Um. No. Doesn't he normally get home at four?"

Mom pressed her lips to the edge of her coffee cup. Coffee? Mom was a teetotaler, even when it came to caffeine. I had never seen her drink coffee, except for in the few weeks surrounding Dad's death. Especially not strong black coffee like the smell wafting from her mug.

"Yes," she said shortly. She took a sip.

"And he hasn't gotten home yet?"

She shook her head. Her forehead was wrinkled with worry, and I could almost feel the knotted tension in her shoulders from here.

The hair on the back of my neck stood up. Oh God. Something was wrong. I knew it. Mom always had a sixth sense about these things. And she was terrible at hiding it.

"Are you sure he didn't wait around for you?" Mom asked. She glanced upstairs, towards Cal's bedroom. "Maybe he was going to walk home with you? Are you really sure you don't know where he is, honey?"

"Mom, is something wrong?"

"No," she said too quickly.

Mom took another sip of coffee. A really long, thoughtful sip that made it obvious she was lying.

"Alright. Fine," I said, scooping my backpack back up and planting a hand on my hip. "Then why do you need him home so badly?"

"We need to talk."

Ouch. That never meant something good. That was a constant phrase around this house when Dad was dying, and I had developed an allergic reaction to it by now.

"About what?"

"About family things."

"Family things like…"

"Things." The coffee mug clinked against the granite countertop as she put it down. "Are you sure you don't know where he is? This is important, Natalie."

"I'm sure." I started toward the hall, but halted. "Mom … does this have to do with James?"

Her hand slipped, letting a drop of coffee jump from the edge of the mug and hit the floor with a splat.

Mom pretended to have not noticed, turning away from me.

"It has to do with the family. We're not talking until the whole family is here."

"Mom."

"We'll talk later. Forget it."

"Fine, Mom," I said, striding out of the kitchen with my backpack strategically placed in front of my pocket. Hidden from view, my hand slipped into my pocket and grabbed my phone. Whatever was going on, it was not good.

Very, very not good.

I threw my backpack on the bed and texted Cal:

NAT:
WHERE ARE YOU???

Ten minutes passed. No answer. I pulled off my shoes and laid back on the bed, ignoring the turning in my gut.

NAT:
THIS ISN'T FUNNY CAL.

MOM IS REALLY REALLY WORRIED.

STILL AT SCHOOL? SETTING DUMPSTER FIRES? IN JAIL?

Fifteen minutes passed. No answer.

NAT:
CAL. ANSWER ME GODDAMNIT.

I had just hit the ten minute mark again and was about to text him again when my screen lit up. Finally, an answer. I grabbed the phone but was surprised to see it was a text from Jess, not from Cal. And it didn't look too good.

JESS:
HOLY CRAP DID YOU SEE IT
WERE YOU THERE

JESS:
NAT ARE YOU OKAY
PLEASE PLEASE PLEASE ANSWER ME

My heart raced. What?

NAT:
I DON'T KNOW WHAT YOU MEAN.

JESS:
OH GOD, ARE YOU SERIOUS

NAT:
YES.

JESS:
I THOUGHT YOU WOULD HAVE KNOWN
BY NOW...

JESS:
OH GOD, NAT, THIS IS BAD
THIS IS REALLY, REALLY BAD

My heart thudded in my chest, and I could feel a cold sweat wash over me. Frustrated, I picked the phone up to dial her number. Jess was terrible at texting. If my world was about to collapse, I needed to know what was going on.

But I didn't get the chance to call her.

Because at that moment, I was distracted by the sound of a ceramic mug hitting the floor and shattering.

"Oh my God," my mother's horrified voice called.

Shit, shit, shit, shit, shit.

Please don't let Cal have done something stupid.

Though I knew that was a useless wish.

I raced downstairs to see my mother frozen in the kitchen, our old landline phone pressed to her ear and the shattered remains of the coffee mug at her feet. Coffee stained her perfect white shoes, and her eyes were as wide as the dinner plates in the sink behind her.

"Mom?" I asked in a small voice.

She seemed paralyzed at the phone, not noticing me. She nodded to herself as she listened to the person on the other line. She licked her lips—her worst nervous tick, the one she only did when things were catastrophically bad.

"No, his father isn't here," she rasped into the phone.

Oh God, Cal. What have you done?

"Mom." My hands shook, and I leaned against the kitchen table to keep myself from keeling over. "Mom, please. What is it?"

"Is he ... is he too badly hurt?" Mom asked.

No, no, no.

"Mommy."

"I ... I don't know where his father is." Mom's eyes sank closed. "No. I'll pick him up myself."

"Mom!"

"I'll be there in thirty minutes."

Mom ended the call and stared at the floor.

"Mom, please," I whispered hoarsely.

Mom's head finally snapped back to me. Her face was white. "Oh, Nat," she moaned.

"What happened?"

"Callum was arrested about an hour ago. There was ... there was a fight with another boy at school. There was a lot of blood, Natalie." Her face fell into her hands. "I knew this was a terrible idea, I knew I

144

shouldn't have married him, Nat. I knew I shouldn't have brought either of them into the house…."

I couldn't hear her droning on about hating the both of them or about how they were both the same violent man. I couldn't hear anything but the deafening buzzing in my ears.

Cal was in jail.

Cal had assaulted someone—and it wasn't hard to figure out who that someone was.

Cal was in trouble. The kind of trouble he couldn't talk himself out of, the kind that had consequences. And there was no way to escape the fact that our lives had just completely changed, even if I didn't know what that meant at the time.

I closed my eyes and took a deep breath as my world collapsed around me.

Bella Scully

CHAPTER 16

By the time we got to the local county jail, Mom had dried her panic tears. But I was still frozen in shock. Once we parked, I only barely managed to stumble out of the car, still clutching my phone in one hand with white knuckles. I was unable to think of anything besides the horrific image I had in my head of Cal, covered in blood, locked in a jail cell.

I struggled to keep my breaths calm.

This could not be happening.

But it was.

"You're lucky they didn't press charges," grumbled one of the guards as he brought the handcuffed Cal out. My head snapped up to see him, ignoring the cold air of the jail and night sounds buzzing outside the window. Oh God, he was bloody. By now the maroon stains that splattered his clothes had turned brown, but I could still smell the faint scent of sour copper. Cal's face was still smudged with red too.

His gaze darted to me where I stood behind my mother, my face white and my hands shaking. He looked down at the floor. He mouthed something at me. I think it was 'sorry.'

"Who was it?" Mom asked, clutching her purse to her chest. Her phone beeped again. James had been texting her nonstop for the last hour, but not once had she checked her phone. Important, but I couldn't pay attention long enough to figure out what it meant. All I could think about was Cal. "Who did he attack?"

"Nathaniel Poole," said another one of the men. "Another student at the high school."

My stomach dropped. Of course, I had to have known that that's who it was. But it was still horrible to hear it.

I wanted Nate to pay for what he had done—but not if it meant Cal wasting his life in some grand gesture for me.

Mom grabbed Cal by the sleeve, then immediately let go when she heard the crunch of dried blood under her hand. She gagged as she wiped the dry flakes off on her jeans.

"Let's go," she said flatly.

"I—" he started, staring at me with pain in his eyes.

"Stop." Mom's tone was entirely cold. She refused to look at him. "Save it. Your father is coming home."

Shit.

***

"Why did you do it?" I asked him once we were home. It was nearly midnight by now, and we were still waiting for James' arrival. Cal and I sat under the dim lights at the kitchen table, both of us clutching mugs of coffee. I had already offered to try smuggling him out of here before James arrived, but he just shook his head.

"For you, Nat."

His voice was painfully soft and hurt.

"You know I didn't want you to start a fight."

"I didn't."

"Explain."

Cal groaned and dropped his head. "He attacked me, Nat. I saw him waiting for you after school. Knew he wanted to hurt you. Couldn't let that happen. He tried going after you when you left campus, which is when I stepped in. He got pissed. He attacked me."

"And you slit his throat?" I hissed, gesturing at his bloody shirt. I couldn't pretend that I didn't appreciate the Batman level protection. But I didn't have to pretend to hate the fact that he was covered in my ex-boyfriend's blood.

"It's not his blood, Nat," he said softly.

"What?"

Cal peeled back one of his many bandages, this one on his forehead above the right eye. I gasped and covered my mouth. Jesus, that was bad.

"He cut you?"

"It's not as bad as it looks. Just bleeds a lot." He patted the bandage back down.

"So…"

"I didn't hurt him. Because I know you didn't want me to. Even if he fucking deserves it."

I stared into my coffee mug for a moment. Well, crap. I hadn't expected that. My fingers crawled to his, and instinctively, he clasped my hand.

"I'm sorry it happened, Nat." He brought my fingers to his mouth and kissed them. "I tried to avoid it. It's fucked up."

Fucked up. A good summary of the evening.

"He's fine," Cal said. "It's why he didn't bother going after me legally. And anyway, it lets him seem like a hero. The good overachieving hero taking pity on the poor fuck up, right?"

"Where is my son?"

James voice echoed throughout the room, harsh and bellowing. I heard my mother's footsteps scurrying in from her bedroom, and James' footsteps stomping to the kitchen.

Cal winced.

I squeezed his hand, then let it slip out of his grip. I wanted so bad to hold him, to protect him from his father like he protected me from Nate. But maybe part of really protecting each other was knowing when to pick our battles. Stepping in would only make it worse. Especially now.

"Is he going to hurt you?" I asked in a small voice. I didn't know what to do. I had pepper spray in my purse, and my hand felt its way inside. It wasn't a lot, but at least it would give him time to run. I could put up with James until then.

"No. He won't, at least not in front of your mother."

James appeared in the doorway. His face was bright red with rage, and his hands were clenched into fists at his side. A vein popped in his forehead. Beside him, my mother poked her head into the kitchen. Worry was etched across her face.

"What. The. Hell. Do you think you were doing?" James growled, stalking forward. Cal stood, and I felt his arm subtly move in front of me. Shielding me again. Like always.

"I asked you a question, you son of a bitch!"

"James, don't talk to him like that," my mother said softly. She reached forward to touch his shoulder, but hesitated. The hatred was radiating from him now. Maybe she was finally seeing who he really was. Her gaze flitted to Cal, suddenly softer and more concerned.

"Don't tell me how to talk to my own son, goddamnit!"

"Don't talk to her like that!" Cal yelled.

Mom was really taken aback at that. Her gaze flitted from James to Cal and back again. Second thoughts, maybe?

"Stop," I said, standing up. James ignored me, but Cal glanced back at me. His gaze was concerned— Don't involve yourself if it will put you in danger. Please, sweetheart.

I had to.

"You said we were going to have a talk," I said to Mom. "That's why we were waiting down here. That's why we were waiting for James to get home. Just tell us what we need to hear before we start fighting, alright?"

James bristled at the mention of 'a talk.'

Hm. Strange. But as long as it kept him from screaming at Cal for a few moments, I would take it.

Mom sat down. "You're right, honey. I think that's really all we can do at this point. Especially after..." She glanced at Cal's bloody shirt, then sighed and put her face in her hands.

"Right. A talk," James spat. He glared at Mom, then pulled out a chair with a screech and fell into it beside her. He was enraged, but there was something else there. They had been keeping a secret from us, hadn't they?

What were they planning?

"We might as well get to the point," Mom said, pulling her face out of her hands and resting her chin on her fingertips. God, she looked tired. Tired and old. These last few months had aged her even worse than Dad's death. A shithead for a husband will do that, I heard.

Cal glanced at her. "Which is….?"

"We're getting a divorce."

You could have heard a pin drop.

Cal's hand tightened on my knee.

"A divorce," I repeated numbly.

Only, I didn't say it. I mouthed the words. I was too weak to put any real voice into it.

I knew their marriage was fucked up. The screaming matches were a testament to that. But there had been no sign that they would actually … well, split up. Mom wasn't a quitter, even if she really should be sometimes. And I got the sense that James despised the idea of failing at anything.

It must have been even worse than I thought.

"We've been thinking about it for a long time," James said coldly. "We think it's best for both of us—all of us—if we separate. Callum and I will do much better living on our own—"

"You're moving out?" I cried.

James shot me a glare. "—living on our own, moving out of this house, yes. It's better for all of us, you in particular. Healthier."

"You mean easier to beat your child you son of a bitch!"

Both James' and my mother's jaws dropped. Cal's hand bit harder into my knee, more out of shock than to hush me.

"Natalie Amelia!" my mother gasped.

I shouldn't have said it. But I didn't regret it.

"That's it," my mother said, standing again. She slapped the table top with a harsh smack. "That's why they're moving out, Natalie! My daughter never used to talk to me that way."

"I told you," James growled, glaring at his son across the table. "I warned you that he ruins whatever he touches."

"Don't fucking talk about him like that!"

"Natalie Amelia Harlow, you will not raise your voice in this house," my mother cried.

"Not if he's going to hurt Cal!"

"And what about Cal hurting you, hm?" My mother shook her head wildly. "Do you have any idea how much you've changed since he moved in, Natalie? You've lost your boyfriend. I've heard you skipped a class last week. Your grades are slipping. You got a B in math last report card! You used to be so good, Nat, and ever since he moved in … ever since we shook up the household, you've changed." She touched my shoulder. "It's for your own good."

I couldn't hear a word of that monologue. I was deafened by the horror of what was going on. They were taking Cal from me. They were taking Cal from me, they were going to hurt him, they were pretending it was good for us.

"So I'll work harder!" I said. "I'll get my grades up. I'll help Cal in school, I'll—"

"Cal has been expelled," James spat. "Funny, the school doesn't want around a thug who assaults its students. Who would have thought. Which is another reason we have to leave. I have to find a school stupid enough to take my son."

"Don't talk about him like that!"

"Stop, Natalie!" said Mom. "We are not discussing this!"

I realized hot tears were staining their way down my cheeks. Cal's shaking hand reached for me, but I stood up.

"No!" I sobbed. "You can't! You can't just—just tear us apart like this! It's not fair!"

"Natalie Amelia, control yourself!"

I tore myself away from her grasp, but she grabbed my sleeve. "Natalie, you have to understand that this is better for all of us. Cal needs help, help he can only get if he's taken away from the distractions here. And you, Nat! You've changed so much since he moved in!"

"It's because I don't have to pretend anymore! I don't have to lie!"

"Bullshit, Natalie!" Even in the midst of my meltdown, my eyes popped open. My mother had never, even in all her fights with Dad, used a curse word. It was anathema to her. "We're not discussing this. He's moving out. James is moving out. We're getting a divorce. This conversation is over."

My mother grabbed her housecoat and stormed out of the kitchen. The slam of the bedroom door reverberated in the walls. Cal was still silent, avoiding looking into his father's eyes. James glared at him hard, but he kept his arms crossed. No more screaming. No more hitting. At least not tonight.

"We're moving out on Friday," James said shortly.

"No," I choked.

"Make sure your things are packed."

"No!"

"I'm sorry this little experiment didn't work, Natalie. But some families aren't meant to be together." He was back to Fake James, the disgustingly personable James with veneers and a bad tan. Pretending to be my friend. I hated him.

"Make sure to get your goodbyes done," he said as he stalked out. "If anyone cares about you enough to want one."

CHAPTER 17

On Friday morning, the crowds of hired hands arrived to begin packing. Callum and his father waited on our lawn, the exhaust of their truck blackening the cloudy sky. Mom had pushed an umbrella into my hands and pulled a rain poncho over me as we watched the crowd of people slosh through the mud to pack boxes into the U-Haul. Everything about that day was horrible—even the weather.

My grandmother used to tell me that rain is God crying.

If so, I appreciated the sympathy.

"Do you know where you're moving?" I asked Cal as we shoved a box into the truck. It held the sheets from his now empty bedroom. Something about how bare the room was now made me sick to my stomach.

"No." He gritted his teeth. "He won't tell me."

"Is it because…."

"Because he wants to hurt me. And because he doesn't want me to talk to you. You know too much about us."

"I hate him."

"I hate him too, sweetheart." He sighed and embraced me. I bit my bottom lip and glanced over his shoulder toward the crowd. No one was looking, but I wasn't sure how much private time we had left. "I'd be lying if I said I wasn't happy to get him away from you. You're too good for him. For us."

"Don't you dare say that."

He shrugged. "It's true."

"I will never be good enough for you, Cal Gatlin."

I hated the sight of the house slowly being emptied. It meant that it was getting closer to the time when they'd take Cal from me. And that thought was unbearable.

When it was almost noon and most of the vans had been loaded, Cal took me by the hand. While everyone else was distracted with finishing the last few vans, Cal pulled me into the kitchen. I glanced out the window as he wrapped his arms around me. Outside in the rain, Mom and James snapped at each other as they repacked a box that had fallen from the van. I had never seen her so angry as I had these last few weeks. Maybe there was a bad influence in the house.

But it wasn't Cal.

"Sweetheart," he whispered, pressing his lips against my ear. "Stop worrying. You look half dead."

"They're taking you away from me, Cal." I cupped his cheek with my palm, loving the way his stubble bit into it. He closed his eyes and rested his face in my hand. God, he was beautiful when he did that. "How will I know if you're safe?"

"I can take care of myself, Nat. I've done it my whole life."

"But how will I know that?" I felt the sobs rise up my chest again, but I crushed them down. I couldn't let my emotions get the better of me. Not today. Not with Cal in danger. "You know he won't let me talk to you. He wants nothing to do with us anymore, not now that we've wrecked his happy little family fantasy. Not now that I know what he is."

"Jesus, Nat," he breathed.

"What? Did I say something wrong? I'm ruining this whole day, I know. I'm sorry."

"No, sweetheart. It's just … I forgot what it was like to have somebody care about me."

Oh God, Cal. Keep digging that knife into my

heart.

"I'll be fine," he said, opening his eyes again. He leaned forward to kiss me long and soft. "I always have been."

"I won't be. Not without you."

"You were fine your whole life without me."

"But I'll miss you. They're stealing you from me, Cal. We haven't even got the chance to really be together." I buried my face in his chest. "We haven't been able to date openly, or go to prom together, or...." I could feel the heat reach my cheeks.

"Make love?" he asked.

"Ugh. It sounds so ... soppy."

"Too bad," he chuckled. "I couldn't just fuck you, Nat. Not you, sweetheart." His fingers combed through my hair.

"Not like it matters now," I mumbled into his chest.

Calls came from outside. The last van had been packed up. James had started corralling and paying the hired hands. They would leave at any moment, regardless of the storm. Or how much it hurt Cal and I to lose each other.

"Listen, Natalie," he said, embracing me harder. "We don't have much time. You need to listen to me, alright sweetheart? Nate is fucking dangerous. And he wants you."

"Fuck him, I don't care."

"But he does. Please, Nat, you have to promise me

you'll be careful. If anything ever happened to you...."

His voice broke.

"I promise," I mumbled into his chest. I couldn't deny him anything. Not Cal. And especially not now.

"Good girl."

He kissed my forehead.

"Now look at me," he ordered.

I lifted my head and looked into his eyes. He brushed the hair from my face. "Fuck, you're beautiful, Nat."

James yelled from outside for Cal to get in the truck.

"Kiss me," he said. "Make it count."

I opened my mouth. His lips pressed against mine, hard and insistent. I knotted my fingers in his hair, pulling him against me. God, I needed him. I always needed him. His tongue slipped into my mouth, and his fingers dug into my back. Another yell from James sounded from the window.

Cal's lips pulled away from me. He cupped my chin and looked into my eyes, serious and intense.

"I will be back," he murmured. His lips pressed against my forehead again, their warmth protecting me from the biting cold of the air around us. His strong arms wrapped around me, the fingers digging into my soft flesh as if he wanted to anchor himself to me and never let go. "I will protect you, Nat. They can take out of the same house, but they can't take me away from you."

"I don't want you to go," I whispered.

"Fuck, Nat. You know I don't want to either." He kissed me hard again, ignoring another of James' yells. "But look." He touched my earring. "As long as you have this, I'm with you. Alright, sweetheart."

"I'll never take it off."

"I know you won't, baby."

His voice broke on the last word. It killed something inside of me, something secret and precious. Something that had died once before with Dad but he had revived in me for just a fleeting moment. Cal had given me something to live for. Now that he was gone, I couldn't see the point of it all. Not now.

He pulled away from me, forcing my arms off of him. I knew he had to go, even if I hated it. "Just listen. Okay?"

I nodded.

"I will promise you this, Natalie Harlow."

His lips pressed against my knuckles, the rough grain of his five o'clock shadow scratching them. I prayed fiercely that it would leave a mark, that I would have something of him left to take to bed with me when I fell asleep crying that night.

"I will come back for you," he said, looking into my eyes. "No matter what. No matter how long it takes. No matter how hard it is. I will fucking come back for you, Natalie Harlow. Because you are worth it."

He kissed my forehead one more time.

"I love you," he whispered.

And then he turned around and walked out of the house, into the car, leaving me shaking and sobbing in the kitchen.

Just as suddenly as he forced his way into my life, Callum Gatlin left.

Once again, I was alone.

Bella Scully

CHAPTER 18

"Natalie. Natalie, open the door."

I pulled the pillow tighter over my head, hoping the feather stuffing would drown my mother's voice out. The rain hammered against my bedroom window, but I could still hear her visiting every few minutes. She pounded on the door again.

"Natalie, please talk to me."

I heard the rattle of the doorknob, but it had been locked ever since Cal left. I knew I shouldn't be this horrible to my own mother. I knew I was being selfish. But God, it hurt.

Mom's frustrated sigh groaned against the door. Her footsteps padded away. Even she was giving up on me.

My face was still hot and wet from the tears that were soaking my sheets. I wasn't sure if it was night yet or not. I hadn't peeked my head out of the covers since I dove under them hours ago, as soon as Cal left and I could think straight enough to climb upstairs. The only thing I could think about, the only thing I could feel, was the crippling pain in my chest. I took a deep breath and touched the diamond stud still clipped in my ear. It was the only thing keeping me sane.

My phone vibrated against my thigh.

Wiping a tear away from my eye, I pulled it out of my pocket and sat up in bed. I glanced at the window, where the moon shined bright and white in the black sky. Cal was long gone by now. I wondered where to.

I glanced at the phone.

NEW MESSAGE FROM
NATHANIEL POOLE

Fuck him.

I deleted it without reading it.

I collapsed back on the bed.

Four hours ago, I had texted Cal. Asking him where he was, if he knew where he was going. No answer.

Three hours ago, I had texted Cal. Asking him if he had gotten my last text. Asking if he had anything to say. No answer.

Two hours ago, I had texted Cal. Asking him to please answer me, to say anything. No answer.

One hour ago, I had gotten a text from Cal's number:

CAL:
DO NOT CONTACT MY SON AGAIN

God, I hated that man.

My phone vibrated. Another text from Nate. I deleted it. In the kitchen beneath my room, the Mom's spoon tinkled against her mug as she fixed herself a cup of strong, black coffee. I was happy that he was away from her, at least.

I had a weekend to wallow. Then school on Monday, where my psycho ex would be waiting for me. Then prom on Saturday, where I would be painfully reminded by the diamond stud in my ear that the only one I loved wouldn't be taking me.

I fell back in bed and pulled the covers over me as I groaned into the pillow. I could keep pretending that this wasn't happening, or I could fix it. I knew I would have to face reality on Monday.

But for now, I just needed to cry.

I choked a new sob into my pillow.

I love you, Cal.

And I miss you so fucking much.

CHAPTER 19

"Did you hear about what happened?"

"Of course I did, Jess. He's my stepbrother."

Don't get choked up. Not in the school hallway, not with so many people around. It's time to stop crying. You got your chance to be weak. Now it's time to be strong.

For Cal.

That immediately rid me of my tears.

It was Monday, the first day back in the real world and out of the prison of my bedroom. Cal had not answered my texts. I had accepted by now that his father had taken his phone.

And I had apologized to Mom for shutting her out. I hated that I was missing Cal. But it wasn't her fault that James was evil. And it especially wasn't her fault for wanting him out of her house, even if she didn't fully understand the situation.

Now that the home was taken care of, it was time to face school. And, as much as I hated to admit it, Nate.

Ugh.

"And where is your bodyguard?" Jess asked me, leaning against my locker. I glanced at the clock. The day was almost over, and still no sight of Nate. Maybe I was getting lucky.

"Gone."

"Gone where?"

"I don't want to talk about it."

Her face softened. "You haven't been answering my texts. Is everything alright with you and Cal?"

"No."

Jess recoiled at my sharp tone. I sighed.

"I'm sorry," I said, rubbing my temples. "I really am. It's just that … Cal moved out. And I hate Nate. And the end of the semester is really starting to get to me. It's a lot to deal with."

"They took your boyfriend from you?"

"Nate isn't my boyfriend anymore."

"I wasn't talking about him."

I froze. "You know?"

Jess stared at me like I was an idiot.

"Jesus, Natalie. Of course I know. What kind of shitty best friend would I be if I didn't? Have you seen the way you two look at each other?"

Don't get choked up, don't get choked up.

"Oh," I said in a small voice.

I kept my eyes fixed on the ground, fighting back the tears as I remembered how warm he felt kissing me moments before he left. I wouldn't cry. I knew that. It was time to be strong.

But it still hurt.

"I'm here for you, Nat," Jess said, squeezing my hand. "Even if you don't know it. And you know he still is, regardless of where he is."

I nodded.

Jess's fingers squeezed around my hand. After a moment, I realized it was too hard to just be reassurance. When I glanced up, she was glaring hard across the hallway at me.

"So I guess this means he's lying," she spat.

I followed her gaze to where Nate was leaning against a locker, watching us. My heart sank.

I guess my good luck couldn't last forever.

"What has he been saying?"

"That Cal tried to attack you. And that he saved you."

"What!?"

"I know." She frowned harder. "I didn't believe it."

The weakness that made my throat close up and hands shake a moment ago washed away. Now I was pissed. Take Cal away from me, and I'll be hurt. Hurt Cal, and I'll kill you.

I spun on my heel and marched to Nate, ignoring Jess's calls from behind me. I knew this was stupid. I shouldn't make a scene, I shouldn't put myself in danger like this. I had made a promise to Cal that I would be careful.

But that was before I knew what Nate was up to.

That was before I started seeing red.

"What the hell do you think you're doing?" I hissed at him, getting as close to his face as possible so he could see the fire in my eyes. "You think you're so fucking clever, don't you? You think you can turn everyone against him so easy?"

"I don't have to," he said coolly, looking down at me. "Everyone already hates him. They know what a fuck up he is."

Fuck up.

I hated that phrase.

"Don't you dare talk about him like that. The only fuck up here is you." My lip curled. "You attacked him. I know what happened Nate. And I swear to God I will tell everyone."

"And who will believe you?"

Ugh. I knew he was right. But I couldn't let him know that. Instead, I leaned forward, glaring even harder.

"Why did you attack him? Because he didn't let you get to me? Why are you so obsessed with me?"

"I want you back, Nat. We're perfect together."

He leaned forward, his eyes oddly earnest. But now that I knew what kind of man he really was, I knew it was he only cared about things being perfect for himself. We looked perfect. The real us was anything but. But Nate was obsessed with looks.

I realized he reminded me of James.

"You will never have me back."

"Natalie—"

He leaned forward to grab my wrist. In that moment, I couldn't stop myself. I would never let him touch me again. I reached forward and slapped him sharply against the face.

He reeled back. I had never hit him back like that.

"Don't ever come near me again," I spat.

I realized the hall around us had gone quiet. Every head in the hall had turned to us, leaving me glaring hard at my ex with shaking hands that had balled into fists at my side. Nate didn't react. He couldn't, not with so many witnesses.

But I could see it in his eyes.

I had gone too far. He couldn't let me get away with that. And in his own little world, he was going to make things right.

I'm sorry, Cal, I thought, realizing I had gotten awfully close to putting myself in danger. But I couldn't regret it.

I turned around to march away before I did anything else extremely stupid. My path was blocked by a huge, hulking figure. My gaze traveled up from the broad chest to the disappointed, grimacing face of Officer Furst.

"Miss Harlow, did you just put a hand to another student?"

"I…"

I panicked, glancing around the hallway. Even a few teachers had peeked their heads out of their doorways to watch the freak show. Good Natalie Harlow, punching her "boyfriend"? Now that made good gossip.

"Miss Harlow, I need you to come with me."

Well, shit.

CHAPTER 20

"Suspended," Mom said with her face in her hands. We sat at the kitchen table a little after sunset, Mom still holding the phone that had just delivered the news. She was drinking coffee again, which was how I knew this was bad.

I sat silently in the chair, looking at the hands folded in my lap. I could handle Angry Mom. I could handle Frustrated Mom. I really, really, really couldn't handle Disappointed Mom.

"Suspended. You hit another student, and you got yourself suspended. Do you have any idea how disappointed I am in you right now?"

"I'm sorry, Mom."

"Natalie, honestly. What has gotten into you?"

"Nothing."

"Nat," she moaned. "You slapped someone. You've never laid a hand on anyone before! You've just gotten yourself suspended. The Natalie I know would never get suspended."

"Maybe the Natalie you know isn't the real Natalie," I said too harshly. I hated how immature I sounded.

But it was true. I was so tired of always being perfect. Cal had allowed me to be myself, even if it was just for the short time that I had known him. I missed it so much.

"This is my fault," Mom groaned, shaking her head. "If I hadn't married James, if I hadn't brought that boy into the house…."

"Mom, it isn't Cal's fault either. He didn't make me like this. He's not a bad guy."

"He beat another student," she spat.

"He didn't, Mom. Have you seen Nate? He's perfectly fine. The worst he has is a scratch on his forehead."

"Natalie, he was arrested."

"And yet Nate didn't press charges. I wonder why."

She frowned. I saw another flash of doubt in her eyes—the same flash of doubt I had seen when James berated Cal in the kitchen. The flash that said, 'Maybe everything James has told me wasn't quite the truth.' 'Maybe Cal isn't as bad as he said.' I hoped she trusted her own daughter more than him.

"I still shouldn't have brought him into the house. You've changed so much, Nat."

"At least he call me a whore," I said too bitterly.

Mom's head snapped up. "What did you say?"

"I heard the screaming matches, Mom. I wasn't already out of the house. I know you two hate other people seeing you being ... imperfect. Not like the Brady Bunch you want to be. But I still heard, Mom. I know how he was."

"Nat... Ugh." She rubbed her temple. "I'm sorry."

"It's fine, Mom. I just want to know that you're okay."

She gave me a sad smile. "I'm supposed to be the adult. I'm supposed to be the mature one who takes care of you. Not the other way around. You're stealing my job, sweetie."

"We're family. We take care of each other."

Mom smiled at me again, but after a moment her expression broke. Mom's head dropped to her hands again.

"Oh God, Nat. I'm sorry. I shouldn't have married him."

"Not your fault." I wanted to squeeze her hand, to comfort her like Jess comforted me. But this was out of my league. Even if I could sympathize with getting roped into a terrible relationship with a terrible man.

"I don't want to pretend to be perfect either, Mom." She glanced up at me.

"You love me even if I'm not, right?"

She sighed. "Of course, Nat. I always love you."

"Even if I got suspended?"

"Oh goodness, Natalie. Of course." She gave me a sad smile and reached across the table to kiss my cheek. "I know it's hard, sweetie. I know you're stressed out. But that doesn't excuse you hurting other people."

"I know," I said, staring into my mug of tea.

"Which is why you're grounded."

"What?" My head snapped up.

"You heard me, Natalie Amelia," she said, standing. She turned on the sink and began scrubbing her now empty mug. "You are not leaving this house. And I'm taking your phone."

"Mom!"

"No. I still love you, Nat. But I am sure as hell not going to allow my daughter to become the kind of person that hits people. You need to learn to grow up."

"Mom, I've got so much to do! I've got to plan for Student Council, I've got to help set up for prom, I've got—"

"Your room, Nat. Now."

I stared at her. This was not how I was expecting this conversation to go. I slipped my phone into my pocket as I stood up.

"I saw that," Mom said without turning around.

Ugh. Mom vision. It sees all.

I put my phone down on the kitchen table.

"Love you, honey," Mom called as I stalked out.

***

It was nearly midnight, and I was still up. Mom, in the midst of an existential crisis brought on by her perfect daughter getting suspended, had forgotten to confiscate my laptop. I had been checking my email obsessively. Part of it was my natural state of workaholicness, aching for something to do to distract me from the train wreck that was my life.

But the other part was desperate for any kind of message from Cal. I doubted he knew my email address...

But it couldn't hurt to obsessively check my account twenty times a day.

After confirming that Cal hadn't emailed me and I was still cut off from him, I closed the laptop and laid back on my bed.

Suspended for a week. No school, Mom slowly descending into madness, and Cal was no longer here to keep me sane. I closed my eyes, trying to remember the taste of him. How warm he would be if he were laying here with me. The gorgeous sound of his deep voice, and what he would say to me if he was here.

It's alright, Nat, he would whisper, kissing my forehead. *Just let me hold you, sweetheart. I'll protect you.*

Or maybe:

Come here, sweetheart. Come here and let me touch you.

Or:

For fuck's sake, Natalie, are you deaf?

Wait, what?

I sat straight up. My imagination was good, but it wasn't nearly good enough to make his voice sound that realistic. And it wasn't good enough to make up the scrabbling noises that scratched against my wall and tapped against the windowsill. My head turned to the window as the bushes below rustled.

My breath caught in my throat.

There was no way.

I waited for a moment.

"I know you heard me, Pink," Cal's voice said in a whisper-shout from outside my window. "Now come on. Open the window before I fall of the side of his goddamn house."

I threw the sheets off and ran to the window.

"Cal?" I whispered, pressing my nose against the glass.

Sure enough, there was Cal Gatlin. Dangling off the side of my house, his fingers grasping at my second-story bedroom window and his foot just barely balancing on the siding. He was still wearing his leather riding jacket, and I could see his bike parked behind the tall bushes around our driveway. His face was blushed and covered in sweat as he scaled the wall of the house to get to me. How he got up there, I'll never know.

All I knew was that I had never been happier.

"You are absolutely crazy," I whispered, a massive smile crawling across my face. I threw up the window and grabbed at his hand. He took it in his, his fingers clasping around mine so naturally that I was sure we were made to be together.

"I know, Pink. Now let me in the house before I fall of this thing. Are you trying to kill me?"

"You're going to kill yourself," I whispered, pulling him in the house. That delicious natural Cal scent washed over me as I watched him brush himself off. His boots were scuffed, he was covered in sweat and dirt, and his hands and arms were bruised and scraped from climbing my house.

He had never looked more gorgeous.

"Yeah, well. It's worth it to see you again."

He turned to me, looking into my eyes for the first time. Oh God, he was real, wasn't he? I wasn't imagining it. He was real, he was Cal Gatlin, he was in my bedroom, and he was finally back home to me.

I couldn't stop myself. I opened my arms and ran to him.

"Oof!" Cal cried as I knocked him over. I wrapped my arms around him as we rolled into the floor, burying my face into his chest. Tears began running down my face.

"Oh God, Cal! You're back! You came back!"

"Hush, sweetheart. Your mom will hear."

"Oh, Cal."

His arms wrapped around me, his fingers digging into the soft skin of my back. His mouth found mine, and his tongue traced my lips again just like it always did. "Oh sweetheart," he whispered. "I forgot how good you taste."

"I thought I lost you, Cal," I choked.

"Oh God, Nat. Don't cry. You know I can't stand to see you cry."

He wiped the tear stain trails from my cheeks and held my chin up for another kiss. I took in a deep breath, inhaling his scent. He smelled perfect. He was perfect. I knew I could never be separated from him now. Before, I could survive. It hurt to lose him, but I could survive. But now? After losing him and having him miraculously return to me?

It would have broken me.

"I promised I would come back for you, Natalie," he whispered against my ear. He kissed my temple. "I don't break promises. Especially not ones I made to you."

"I know, Cal." I buried my face into his neck. "I know."

We laid together on my bedroom floor, our chests rising and falling together. The sound of Mom's soft snores drifted through the walls, assuring us that we were safe for the moment. Cal's fingers combed through my blonde hair.

"How did you get away?" I whispered.

"He's sleeping. He doesn't care what I do as long as it doesn't cause trouble for him. He doesn't pay attention to me. All I had to do was take the bike and go once I figured out where we were and how I could get to you, Nat."

"But he's going to realize that you're gone."

"Yes."

"You don't sound too worried about that."

"Because I have a plan."

His voice sounded dangerously sure of itself. I glanced up at him with trepidation, my gaze searching his face. He looked down at me coolly, not a single worry apparent in his expression. Cocky Cal—I loved that. But it was dangerous.

"Alright. Fine. What craziness have you gotten yourself into? And does it break any major laws?"

"Nope. Well, maybe."

I groaned. He smiled and kissed my forehead again.

"I've gotten a motel room downtown. I know he'll probably figure out that I've gone back to this town. But honestly? As long as I'm out of his hair, I doubt he'll care. I can lay low, Nat. And I can take care of myself. I told you. I'm good at that. And if it allows me to be near you?"

He kissed me.

"Well, I'll do anything for that," he whispered against my mouth. He nuzzled my neck, making me moan. "Quiet, sweetheart. Quiet. Your mom will hear us."

"Take me with you."

"What?"

Cal pulled back, still cupping my face. His jaw had dropped, and his eyes were wide. A smug part of my took pride in the fact that I was still able to shock Cal Gatlin. He shook his head, running his fingers along my face as he cradled it.

"No. You've got school, and—"

"I don't. I was suspended," I said, beaming.

He was silent.

"Say something, please. Did I give you a heart attack?"

"You? Suspended?"

"You sound like my mom."

"You're Natalie Harlow. You don't get suspended."

"Well, I did. And Mom is used to me being a drama queen, so I doubt she'll expect me to leave my room, which means she'll never suspect I'm gone. It's perfect." I leaned forward and kissed him. "Please. Take me with you. I need to be with you, Cal. Being away from you…."

My voice broke.

"I can't," I whispered, unable to summon the strength to speak. "Please, Cal, I can't be away from you again."

His fingers drifted from my cheek to the ear where his earring was still clipped. I hadn't taken it off since he left.

He nodded.

"You know I can never say no to you, Nat." He gave me a cheeky smile and kissed me again. "So come on. Let's go."

He took my hand, and we ran away from home.

CHAPTER 21

Cal and I lied on the bed in his motel room, holding each other's bodies and looking into each other's eyes. By now, it was nearly three in the morning. Mom would still be sleeping, not knowing that her daughter had escaped out her window with her criminal stepbrother. James probably didn't know that Cal was gone. Or, more importantly, he probably didn't care.

Cal kissed me. "I love you, Nat."

"You know I love you," I said.

"How did you get suspended?" he asked me after a moment. He straightened up on the bed and kicked away the half empty pizza box at the edge of it, the one we had ordered an hour ago. His arm wrapped around my waist and brought me to sit up with him. Our legs intertwined together.

"I hit someone."

His eyes widened. "You?"

"Yeah."

"I don't believe it."

"That someone was Nate."

His eyes closed. "Now I believe it. But I wish I didn't."

"He deserved it."

"I'm not arguing that, Nat. What I'm worried about is the fact that you're underestimating him. He's not stupid, Nat. But he is crazy. And crazy is dangerous. Especially if you're provoking him by attacking him in public."

"I didn't attack him."

His eyes opened, suddenly furious. "Did he come after you? Is that why you had to hit him?"

"No."

"Then why?"

"He…. Well…." I rubbed the back of my neck. "He was talking shit about you. I couldn't let him get away with that."

His eyes rolled dramatically, and he fell back on the pillows. "Nat. You can't do that."

"I couldn't let him lie about you."

"Natalie, it doesn't matter. I'm fine. He can't get to me anymore. But you? He's obsessed with you. You're just hurting yourself by trying to defend me. I'm not worth defending."

"Don't say that. You're always worth defending."

He groaned. "Just please promise me you'll stay away from him, Nat."

I was silent.

"For me."

I sighed. "Oh, fine. Alright. Ugh."

"You're so dramatic, sweetheart," he said, cradling my chin again. He rolled on top of me as he kissed me, his hands resting softly on my waist. His knee rested between my legs, reminding me of that first night that we had kissed. Really, really kissed. The first night I realized I had feelings for him.

"Cal," I moaned against his mouth.

His hands tightened on my waist, and he let the weight of his body press me into the mattress.

"I know, sweetheart. I've missed you too."

"Don't stop," I gasped, knotting my fingers in his hair. He growled a deep, primal sound as he kissed me, reacting to my little moans. His tongue searched my mouth.

"Do you ... do you want..." he groaned. He couldn't push out the whole sentence. His hands shook where they held me, and his breathing was ragged with need.

"Yes," I whimpered. "I need it."

"Fuck, you have no idea," he growled raggedly. "No fucking idea what you do to me... when you make those noises, Nat... fuck." His hips grinded into mine. My panties were soaked already. "I just ... God, I need you, sweetheart."

"Take me. I'm yours."

"Oh sweetheart..."

"I need you, Cal," I breathed into his mouth.

His fingers found the waist of my pajama pants again and pulled them down. His eyes searched my face and his mouth kissed my hungrily. His hands fumbled as he pulled down my panties, too distracted by his burning need for me.

"Spread your legs," he growled.

How could I resist him? With his delicious lips against mine, his stubble scraping my cheek, his fingers feeling their way into my wet panties and pressing against my clit? My head fell back helpless as his hands pulled my thighs apart. His head disappeared down between my legs.

"Cal!" I cried in a sob of passion as his tongue flicked against my clit. His delicious, dark chuckle vibrated against me.

"That's it, sweetheart. Tell me how good you feel."

"Oh Gooooood."

The flat of his tongue stroked against me, slow and gentle. I couldn't stand it—I needed him to make me his, to just ravage me hard and fast.

But he knew that. Which was why we were going slow. He loved to tease me.

Damn him, I thought.

Until his tongue slipped inside me, and I couldn't think anything.

"Don't stop!" I whimpered. His tongue lashed against me harder now, sensing my urgency. He drank me deep, exploring every inch of my pussy before coming back to my clit and sucking hard. Helpless whimpers escaped my lips.

"Put your fingers in my hair, sweetheart," he ordered. "Pull my hair. Let me know how much you fucking need me."

I obeyed, and he gasped. "Oh, fuck!"

His sucked harder on my clit. His arms wrapped around my thighs, forcing my pussy onto his face. I panted and squirmed underneath him, but there was no use. Cal wouldn't let me go until I came for him.

Hard.

"You're close, aren't you?" he growled. "Fuck, I can taste it. I know you are, baby. I'm going to lick an orgasm out of that sweet little clit."

I couldn't answer. It was too much. The tension in my body was rising, tightening, growing too intense to handle. I needed release. I pulled Cal's hair, and his tongue whipped against my clit harder.

So close, so close....

"Say my name when you cum," he growled.

It pushed me over the edge.

"Cal!" I cried in a strangled moan.

Cal's fingers bit into my thighs, forcing me to stay on his mouth as I writhed against him. His tongue invaded me, and he sucked hard on my clit. "That's it, sweetheart," he groaned. "Cum on my mouth. Let me taste it. Don't stop."

My fingers shook as I came, pulling Cal against me by his hair. His tongue kept working me, stretching my orgasm out for longer than I had ever experienced. I rode the wave on Cal's tongue, blinded by the pleasure of it. *I love him so much,* I thought to myself helplessly. That realization was the only thing I felt stronger than the pleasure from coming.

I love him, I love him, fuck this feels good, I love him.

By the time it was over, I was a gasping, heaving mess on the bed. Cal's tongue kept stroking me in long, soft licks that brought me down from the high, back to a soft bed of unimaginable pleasure. His head rose from between my thighs, his face still glistening with my wetness.

"Was it good, sweetheart?"

"Yes," I whimpered. God, how could it not be? I wanted desperately to reach over and kiss him, but I couldn't find the strength to sit up. He was good. So, so good. He had totally knocked me out. I could barely find the strength to breathe.

Cal's arms wrapped around me again as he pressed his lips to mine. I could feel his cock straining against his jeans as I pressed his body against me. I needed it, I realized. I needed him, and I needed all of him. His mouth, his kisses, his cock. I needed him so fiercely I thought I might die.

"Please, Cal," I groaned. "Fuck me."

"No."

"Please!" I whimpered.

"Sweetheart," he groaned.

He grabbed my hands, stopping me from ripping the zipper of his jeans down.

"Are you sure?"

"Yes. Please, Cal. I need you."

"Oh, fuck, Nat."

I grabbed his hair and forced his mouth onto mine. He kissed me eagerly, hungrily, tasting every inch of me.

"Please," I moaned into his ear. "I need you."

He looked at me helplessly.

"You know I can't say no to you," he said into my neck, shaking his head. He leaned back and reached for his zipper. "Lay back on the bed. Spread your legs for me, sweetheart."

I let my head fall on the pillows, my soft golden curls fanning out in a halo around my head. Cal pulled a condom from inside his coat jacket, and a giggle bubbled out of me as I remembered the condom he had stuffed in my trumpet years ago as a childhood bully. He raised an eyebrow.

"You can't laugh at it if you haven't even seen it yet," he said, working the button on his jeans.

"You're ridicu—oh."

Cal pulled his cock out from his jeans, already hard and dripping for me. Jesus. He was big.

My eyes traveled from his jeans to his eyes. His eyebrow was still cocked, but there was a knowing smile on his lips.

"Something wrong, Nat?"

"Shut up."

"Love you too, sweetheart," he said, rolling the condom on. I pressed my eyes shut. The initial mouth-watering surprise at his cock was being replaced by a tiny shiver of fear. This might hurt. But at the same time, there was no way in hell I was letting Cal Gatlin know about my little "inexperience" problem. I'd be hearing cherry jokes for the next fifty years.

I bit my lip as Cal's strong hands spread my thighs, leaving me helplessly open to him.

"Jesus, Nat," he whispered, leaning down to kiss me again. His mouth moved down to my right breast, sucking hard on the nipple. "You're so fucking wet, sweetheart."

I groaned as his cock pressed into my leg, hard and warm. Aching to fuck me. One of Cal's fingers slid inside me.

"Oh God!"

Cal's tongue flicked against my nipple. I gasped again. His finger was working my clit, and I wasn't sure how much longer I could hold on. I needed his cock inside me before I came.

"Please, just fuck me."

"You want it?"

"Yes!"

He positioned himself between my legs and pressed the head of his cock against me. I whimpered, and one of my shaking hands grabbed a fistful of the sheets.

"Fuck, Nat, you feel so good."

"I need you, Cal."

"I know, sweetheart. But let's go slow."

He grinded his hips into me. My eyes rolled back into my head as the moans flowed out from my lips. Cal's fingers drifted over my thigh before pulling my leg around him.

His thumb pressed against my clit.

Too much, too close! I needed him now, before he pushed me over the edge again. I wanted to cum with him. I needed it.

"Cal!"

"Tell me what you need, baby."

"I need you!"

"How do you need me?"

"I need you inside me!"

He leaned forward, his cock still positioned at my entrance. His eyes locked with mine, and he bit his gorgeous lower lip hard. "Tell me, Nat," he growled, his face only an inch from mine. "Say it louder. I can't hear you, baby."

"I need you, Cal," I gasped. He kissed me.

"Need me how?"

"I need you to fuck me."

His lips pulled back into a cruel grin.

"No."

My eyes fluttered open. Cal hovered above me, the weight of his body pressing me into the soft sheets and his warm skin caressing every inch of my own. His thumb pressed hard circles into my clit faster, and little sparks of electricity were already surging through my veins. I felt his cock pressing into me, just enough to tease me, not enough to give me the satisfaction I was desperate for. I looked into his eyes.

"Why?" I whimpered.

"I told you Nat." Another kiss on the neck. I could feel his shit-eating grin against the pulse in my throat. He pressed his lips to my ear. "I can't fuck you."

I gave him a questioning look. He smiled triumphantly and leaned forward, pressing his forehead to mine. I could taste his delicious breath, and I ached to feel his tongue in my mouth.

"I'm going to make love to you."

Oh God.

He had been sexy before. Then, I wanted him.

But now? Now that I looked into his eyes and didn't just see my stepbrother, but the man I loved?

Now I needed him.

"Please, Cal," I whimpered. "Make love to me."

"Oh sweetheart," he groaned, pressing his cock into me.

My nails dug into his back as the delicious pain bit into me. Yet somehow the pain was completely overwhelmed by the pleasure. The aching for Cal that had been killing me had drifted away, replaced by the mind blowing realization that Cal was inside me. Cal was inside me, Cal was fucking me, Cal was making love to me. I buried my face in his shoulder.

Cal's hips moved against mine slowly, grinding against my clit as he fucked me. "Oh—oh—oh!" I gasped.

"Are you alright, sweetheart?" Cal growled into my neck.

"I—I—yes!"

His hips began to speed up, fucking me harder, driven on by his need for me. Cal had begun whispering things in my neck, but I was so overwhelmed the feel of him fucking me that I couldn't make out any of them. His hips bucked against mine hard, and I winced again.

"Ooh, slow down!"

Cal froze. He pulled back, cupping my chin and lifting my face to inspect for a moment. His eyes widened.

"Oh God, Nat. I forgot. You're a virgin, aren't you?"

"I'm fine," I said, wincing.

"Oh, fuck, sweetheart. I'm so sorry."

"No, don't pull out!" I dug my nails into his ass, holding him there. I was already adjusting to his size. The pain had mostly gone by now. What was left was the body wracking need for him, a need that screamed out for him to fuck me into the bed. I needed him to make me his.

"Do you need me to stop?" he breathed raggedly. I could feel his hips trembling. Aching to fuck me senseless, but held back by his fear for me. I shook my head.

"Please, don't stop."

"Nat. Don't just say that because you think you have to."

"Fuck me, Cal." I reached up and touched his face, running my fingers gently along his grizzled cheek. His eyes were burning into mine. Sweat dripped down his temple. He wanted me. He wanted me so fucking bad.

But not as much as I needed him.

"Natalie," he groaned. "Are you ... are you sure?"

I reached up and took his jaw in my hand. I pressed my lips to his, kissing him long and deep. His tongue ran along my lower lip, and I moaned into his mouth.

Then I looked into his eyes.

"Cal," I growled. I put the same passion into my voice that I had that first night, attempting to seduce him into staying in my room. His breath caught. "I need you to fuck me."

"Oh, God, Nat!"

His hips rammed into me, forcing a helpless gasp out of my mouth. Oh, fuck, that was good. Cal buried his face in my neck and hair again as he fucked me hard and fast. "Take it, Nat," he groaned. "Fuck you're so good. Take my cock, sweetheart. Take my cock—take my body—oh, fuck, you're tight. Take everything, baby. It's all for you."

My legs trembled. I was close again. So close.

"Don't stop," I whispered.

He could tell by the way my moans grew louder and more desperate. His hips began thrusting harder into me. His thumb reached between my legs and grinded mercilessly against my clit, drawing the pleasure out of me in quick moans.

"Come on, Nat," he growled. "Come for me, sweetheart."

"Cal," I begged.

"That's it, Nat. You're a good girl, aren't you? Then come for me like a good girl."

"Oh—fuck!"

He drove me over the edge, and I came squirming and screaming into his shoulder. He growled encouragements into my ear as I came. "Fuck, yes, Nat—don't stop—come for me, sweetheart. God, you have no idea how fucking sexy you are when you do that. Dig your nails harder into my back, baby."

I wrapped my legs around him. His thumb massaged circles into clit, drawing the orgasm out longer and harder.

"Oh, God, Cal," I breathed as I floated down from my climax. His hips bucked into me harder as my panting slowed. He was close too, I realized. His arms crushed me to him.

"Oh, fuck Nat."

"Come for me, Cal."

He kissed me hard, pressing his lips to mine so intensely that I was sure they'd be bruised in the morning.

"I love you," I whispered.

He groaned into my lips as he came.

I pulled his lips to mine again as he came down from his own orgasm. "Oh, sweetheart," he groaned into my mouth. "You have no idea how good you are."

He curled his body into mine, pulling my face into his neck again. His arms wrapped around me. He buried his face in my hair and whispered sweet nothings as we drifted to sleep. I sighed contentedly as his fingers combed through my hair again. Finally, we were as close as we were before we were separated. Finally, we were together again.

But this time, nothing could tear us apart.

"I love you," he whispered.

CHAPTER 22

Cal's warm lips kissed along the back of my neck.

"Mmm," I mumbled. His fingers rubbed small circles into my hips where he held me, and his face was buried in my hair. The warmth of our bed and body heat swallowed me. I never wanted to leave. In bed with Cal was where I really belonged, I thought to myself with a sigh of pure satisfaction.

"Are you awake, sweetheart?"

"Mmm hmm."

"Good. Because it's almost 4pm."

"What?!"

Cal smirked as he watched me shoot straight up, one hand clutching at my frazzled hair as I searched for the clock. The numbers 4:13 blared at me in red.

"Oh God," I moaned.

"What's wrong?" he said, kissing my shoulder and down my arm. His fingers intertwined with mine, and he brought my hand to his mouth with a small, warm contented groan.

"Mom. I've been gone since midnight."

"I thought you said we were safe? That she wouldn't worry, she'd just think you were being dramatic?"

"Yes, but … but what if she checks my room?"

"Did you leave the door locked?"

"Oh. Well … yes." I laid back onto the pillows. Cal cuddled next to me, continuing to kiss every inch of my skin. The afterglow was still clinging to us, and every muscle in my body was deliciously sore. Memories of last night came flooding back to me.

Cal's tongue lapping at me until I screamed.

Cal growling 'spread your legs.'

Cal fucking me into the bed.

"Sweetheart?"

"Sorry," I said, rolling into his embrace. "I just get distracted by how sexy you are."

"If you keep stroking my ego, I'll have to fuck you again."

"Yes, please."

I reached for his cock, but he grabbed my hand. "No."

"Ugh. Why not?"

"Because. We've got somewhere to be, remember?"

He rolled his eyes at my confused look. His hand reached forward to touch the diamond stud in my ear.

"Prom, Nat. I told you we were going together, didn't I?"

"Prom? Seriously?" I shook my head. "Cal, I'm supposed to be grounded, and you're supposed to be off in whatever gulag your dad dragged you to. And we're—or at least, we were—step siblings. Family. Do you have any idea what kind of rumors are going to go around if we actually show up?"

"The same kind of rumors that go around when perfect Natalie Harlow slaps her perfect boyfriend Nate?"

"Don't remind me."

"You don't have to be perfect all the time, Nat." He held me tighter. "If they don't love you when you aren't perfect, they don't really love you. So they gossip about it. So fuck them. They didn't deserve you in the first place."

I ran my fingers along his strong arm, tracing the dark lines of his tattoos as they coiled around the muscles.

"Do it, Nat," he urged. "If not for me, then for you. Do it to prove that you don't have to be perfect. Do it to prove that you are just as gorgeous—"

A kiss on my cheek.

"—and sexy—"

A kiss on my neck.

"—and fuckable—"

A kiss on the top of my breast. My heart fluttered. If he kept going down, we wouldn't get out of this bed for a week.

"Alright, alright. I get it," I said.

"… that you're just as good when you're imperfect as when you're pretending to be perfect. I know that, but I don't think you do. Not yet. Do it to prove it to you and to them."

"I don't know. Nate will be there…"

He nuzzled my neck. "If you go to prom with me, I promise that when we get back, I will fuck you so hard you forget your own name."

Oh God.

"Let's go to prom!" I said, throwing off the covers.

***

I struggled with the zipper of the pink taffeta dress, watching my ridiculous self in the mirror. Cal had helped me climb back into my bedroom through the window, allowing me to leave the room for a few minutes to assure Mom that I was still alive in the room. Throwing a tantrum, not dead. Which now left me hopping on one foot, pulling on a fluffy pink prom dress in front of the vanity mirror as Cal waited below in the bushes.

"Come on, Pink."

His whisper-shout sounded from the window. I winced. Mom was going to hear him, and then I really would be dead.

"Hold on," I whisper shouted back.

"You're so slow."

"Oh, for God's sake."

I finally pulled the zipper up, then slipped on my converse. A pebble plinked against the glass of my window, and I sighed. Cal was many wonderful things. Patient was not one of them.

"Alright, calm down, I'm done," I said, throwing the window up. Oh, crap. Climbing up in pajamas was hard. Climbing down in a prom dress? While staying hidden from Mom? Impossible.

"Jump," Cal ordered.

"You're crazy."

"Yes, I am. Now jump."

"I am not breaking my neck. You will not cart my corpse to the morgue in a prom dress."

His overdramatic sigh came from the dark bushes below me. I couldn't even see him. I was not jumping.

"Do you trust me?" his voice asked.

I sighed. Ugh.

I tumbled out of my window with about as much grace as someone in a ball of pink taffeta could manage. My converse kicked through the air as I plummeted to my demise, my curls blinding me as the wind blew them in my face.

"Oof!"

Cal's strong arms wrapped around me as we tumbled back into the bushes. My shook the dizziness from my head. I had knocked Cal flat on his ass, but as far as I could tell, we were both alive. I smiled down at Cal and rubbed a smudge of dirt off his cheek with my thumb. Considering how things in our lives had gone so far, that was a definite accomplishment.

"Come on, Pink," he said, setting me on my feet. He ran his fingers through his hair as he shook his own head.

And then he looked at me for the first time.

"Jeeeesus, Pink."

His jaw was slack again, and his eyes searched me up and down. The same starstruck look he had given me when he had first seen me in Maneater.

He shook his head.

"I'll have to beat the boys off with a stick."

"If I don't die on the way there," I said, eyeing the bike. Once again… pajamas was easy. Prom dress, not so much.

"Do you trust me?" he asked, taking my hand.

"Ugh. You know I do."

He grinned crookedly. "Good." He kissed my hand. "Then I hope you won't be too mad about this."

Before I could fight him off, Cal had swept me off my feet and over his shoulder. I slapped his back as he laughed a delicious deep chuckle. He patted my ass as it struggled in the air.

"Cal, goddamnit!"

"Sorry, sweetheart." His tone was very not sorry. I huffed and crossed my arms from my undignified position tossed over his shoulder. "Now hold on tight. I don't want to ruin that dress."

"You. Are. Terrible."

"And you're beautiful."

He gave my ass a playful spank.

The bike was parked behind the bushes, allowing us a quick getaway with Mom none the wiser once again. He set me right side down on the bike, and I gathered up my skirts and dignity. He mounted the bike and drew my arms around him.

"You really do look beautiful."

"You're an asshat."

"You're so sexy when you're mad."

"I will murder you in your sleep."

He kissed my cheek.

Then he hit the gas. The bike took off with such a jerk that I nearly fell off the back, and a breathless gasp escaped my throat. Cal caught my arms and wrapped them around him, saving me from a pink silk wrapped doom in the middle of the street. I pressed my body against him as tight as possible, mortified at the idea of death by deranged prom date.

"Converse?" he asked as we hit the road. "You're wearing tennis shoes to a dance?"

"Not so beautiful now, am I?"

"You're always beautiful, Pink," he said, locking our fingers together. "Now, come on. Let's go to prom."

CHAPTER 23

"Name?"

"Natalie Harlow."

"And yours?"

"Callum. Callum Gatlin."

The chaperone's eyebrow raised, and his fingers fumbled with the clipboard. He looked from me—my hair frazzled, muddy Converse on my feet, and a ruffled pink dress clinging to my scrawny body—to Cal, who was looking as cool and perfect as ever in his black t-shirt and jeans. Still, not the tux the chaperone was probably expecting. I could already hear his thoughts now:

Nat Harlow?

With Cal Gatlin?

Impossible.

But lately, it seemed like we were doing a lot of impossible things. The chaperone shrugged after checking the list of senior names one last time. "Thought you would have been expelled by now," he said to Cal.

"Oh, I'm not the bad one. Haven't you heard yet?" Cal asked, wrapping an arm around me and pulling me to him. "This one is a troublemaker now. Got herself suspended."

The chaperone rolled his eyes and pushed us through into the crowded gym.

"You're terrible," I whispered.

"Me?" His eyes widened as he gestured to himself innocently. "I have no idea what you're talking about. I'm not the one who got suspended, Nat. I think you're beginning to be a bad influence on me. What if you smudge my flawless reputation?"

I pushed his arm playfully. He swept me up by the waist to kiss me. I could feel a blush creep across my face as he did. The room was dark, only lit by flashing strobe lights, and the music was deafening. The throngs of people were all crowded together, bending to scream in each other's ears over the music. I knew no one could see or hear us.

But it was still a dangerous, delicious thrill to kiss my own stepbrother in public. Especially if that stepbrother was Cal.

"Oh. My. God."

My head whipped around. I could hear the faint sound of Cal's deep, rumbly laugh by my ear through the pounding bass of the pop music. I squinted my eyes through the darkness, just barely making out a brunette bobbing on her feet with wide eyes and a wider smile.

"Oh. My. God!" Jess cried.

"Hush!" I screamed over the music. I could barely hear my own voice, but panic was starting to take over. Jess and Cal ignored me. Both of them had stupidly giddy smiles smeared across their faces. "Jess, are you tipsy?"

"Knew it," she sang. "I. Knew. It. Knew you were together, called it ages ago. Incest is the best, right?"

"Step-incest," I said, swatting her away.

"Bahahaha, this is great. Nate's face is going to be—"

"Nate is here?" I asked, freezing.

"Duh, Nat. He's on student council, remember? It's kind of a rule that he has to be here?"

213

Crap. I didn't expect that. I should have, but in the haze of romantic midnight getaways and sex in motel rooms with my bad boy stepbrother, it may have slipped my mind.

Cal's arm squeezed around me.

"You shouldn't worry," he whispered.

"I know. I'm still going to, though."

"Hm. I'll have to distract you then."

"Cal—no!"

It was too late. Cal had grabbed my arm and was pulling my helpless body onto the dance floor. A few stares followed us, which I knew he loved. Behind us, Jess was bouncing on her toes, screaming something about "oh my god, so romantic."

He wrapped his arm around my waist. "Come on, sweetheart," he said into my ear. "I bet I can distract you."

Yes. Yes he could.

Cal was a crazy good dancer. I had never expected it from him, but I guess it made sense—he loved drinking, women, and being a slut, all of which readily accessible at clubs. After every dance, he would pull me to his chest and yell something sweet into my ear.

"They're watching you," he said once. He nodded at a gaggle of boys chattering amongst themselves as their gaze followed me, twirling along the dance floor with Cal's arms around me.

"They probably think you kidnapped me."

"They think you're beautiful."

"Ugh. Stop."

"It's true, Nat." He pulled me closer for a kiss. "You're beautiful all the time, of course. But right now? Drop dead fucking gorgeous."

I rolled my eyes at him. He grinned and kissed me again.

There may have been a few drinks in between there, too. Not that perfect Natalie Harlow would agree to a little shot of the vodka her stepbrother had smuggled in in a water bottle.

No, definitely not.

It was approaching midnight again, and the party had begun to draw down. By now, Cal was covered in sweat. My Converse had been kicked off and were sitting in a chair at the other end of the gym, ready to be stolen by one of the many drunks around us. Jess had been flitting from boy to boy, seeking out her next victim for the night.

She had invited me once or twice, but the idea of being with anyone but Cal just made me laugh.

I was his, I realized.

I was always his.

"Are you ready to go, sweetheart?" he asked, kissing my forehead. I was swaying in his arms, my cheek pressed against his warm chest, basking in his scent as he led me across the floor. A slow song. One of the last of the night.

"Mm hmm," I mumbled. The thrill of sneaking out, wild dancing with the man I was desperately in love with, and booze that I most definitely did not accept from said man had finally gotten to me. Cal's fingers laced their way into my hair again.

"Alright, come on. I'll carry you."

"Don't," I mumbled into his chest. "People will see."

"Good. I want them to know who's protecting you."

Gently, he lifted me up, carrying me in his arms like a princess. We stopped by the door to grab my shoes and give a goodbye to Jess, who was as definitely not drunk as I was.

"Nat—" she slurred.

"Do you have a ride?" Cal asked, frowning at her. Jess was a sloppy drunk, and she wasn't good at hiding it.

"Chill," she said with an over dramatic eye roll. "This one is driving me home." She jabbed a thumb at a junior girl who was watching her with a distinct air of hero worship. "But I've got to—gotta tell you—crap, what was it?"

"Nate," said the junior softly.

Ugh.

"Oh yeah. Your psycho ex saw you."

"And where is he?" asked Cal tightly.

"Gone. He left."

The tension in Cal's shoulders relaxed. Well, that was … odd. Things were finally working out for Cal and Nat.

"Are you sure?" Cal said.

"Yeah. We watched him drive away. Looked pretty disgusted," Jess said, shaking her head. "Stomped around a lot, made a phone call, left. I guess he figured out he lost. Had to call a ride to get his sorry ass out of here."

"Lost?" I asked.

"Yeah. Lost you. To tall, dark, and murderous over here." Jess slapped him lightly on the bicep. "Have you seen the way you dance?"

"That doesn't mean we're in a relationship."

"Yeah, but those do," she said, pointing at the exposed flesh of Cal's arm under his tight t-shirt. Scratches. Even more were apparent through the stretched-thin cloth over his back. I had really done a number on him last night. "Not hard to figure out you fucked each other's brains out."

The junior girl looked scandalized.

Cal just smiled.

"Thank you, Jessica. Come on sweetheart."

"We didn't—" I stammered.

"Yeah, yeah, I know," Jess said, rolling her eyes again. "You're perfect and chaste and pure as driven snow because that's what good girl Natalie Harlow is supposed to be like." She burped. "Now go home and fuck each other again. You're so much more chill now that you're getting laid."

I buried my red face in Cal's chest as he laughed.

I leaned on Cal as he walked me out to the parking lot. Memories of last night and this night melded together. Cal telling me he loved me. Cal making love to me. Dancing. Fucking. Drinking. Watching others stare at us and realizing I didn't care, that I wanted to be seen with him. Realizing that this night was the happiest I had been in a long time.

It was perfect.

Or so I thought until we got to the parking lot.

"There he is!"

The blinding light of a flashlight hit my eyes. My stomach turned, and I had to suppress my gag reflex as my tipsy self was sent stumbling backwards. Cal's grip on my tightened, keeping me upright. I could sense the tension in his body.

Something was wrong.

"Oh God, Natalie!"

Mom's voice. My bleary eyes blinked themselves open.

A crowd of people was gathering at the front of the school. Mom was in front, and next to her was … oh shit. James. Looking furious. And my old friend, Officer Furst. A crowd of onlookers surrounded them. Another wave of nausea hit me as I realized the cars next to them were from the county police department.

My woozy brain went into panic mode. This could not be good. Cal's hand tightened on me—he knew it too.

"How did they know?" Cal said under his breath.

"Nate," I realized, drunk me having a fleeting moment of clarity. "Jess said he called someone. I knew he wasn't just going to give up. He must have known you weren't supposed to be here—must have known you were sent away … must have called … oh God."

"You mean he called your mother?"

"And … and the cops," I said with a sickening realization. Behind Mom wasn't just her car. There were also a group of cops. And one of them had the flashing red and blue lights of a siren on, reflecting in the puddles over the pavement.

"We haven't done anything illegal."

"Besides supplying alcohol to a minor?"

His jaw locked. "We'll get through this, Nat."

"Natalie, God, are you okay?" Mom was running to me now, her hand clutched over her chest and her purse swinging wildly as she jogged. The crowd followed her. Furst had a death glare fixed on Cal. Cops surrounded him.

No, no, no.

This wasn't happening.

"I'm fine, Mom," I said in a small voice.

She hit me with almost enough force to send me stumbling backwards, her outstretched arms wrapping around me as she started sobbing. Cal's arm instinctively reached forward to steady me, but Mom's furious voice shrieked at him.

"Don't touch my daughter!"

Cal pulled his arm back. His gaze stayed fixed on me, but it wasn't long before his own arm was jerked back by James.

"Cal!"

I reached for him. Mom forced me to stay put.

"Oh God, honey, did he hurt you?"

"Mom, I'm fine. Cal—"

I was desperate to reach him. I could already see the cops surrounding him, and I knew what would happen next. James was stalking forward too, and I couldn't let him hurt Cal. I knew how bad this looked. I knew there was nothing I could do to save him. But, God, I had to try, didn't I?

"I knew it, I knew I shouldn't have brought that boy into the house," she sobbed. "He kidnapped you, didn't he?"

"Mom, no! He didn't hurt me." I turned to the police that were surrounding him. "Please, I chose to go with him. I wasn't kidnapped if I chose to go. You can't—"

"Doesn't matter," said one of the cops. "You're a minor. Gatlin is eighteen. You were taken from your home without your guardian's permission. Legally in this state? Kidnapping."

"No."

"We're taking you home," she said flatly.

"Mom!" I tried to fight against her, but a few of the cops turned to me. I knew I was acting out of character. I knew I was slurring my words. And I knew my head was getting dizzier. I froze as soon as it dawned on me that the police could see that too.

If they were arresting Cal for helping me sneak out, there was no telling what they'd do to him for plying the kidnapped minor with vodka. I couldn't keep drawing attention to myself. Not if it meant hurting Cal even more than I already had.

I stopped fighting. Mom grabbed my arm again and began leading me away. I glanced back at the crowd of police.

"Evening, Gatlin," Furst said, his voice weary. His arms were crossed, his expression grim. "Knew I'd be seeing you again."

Cal grimaced.

For what was probably the billionth time in his life, Cal had a pair of handcuffs slapped on his wrists. I tripped over my own feet as Mom led be away, desperately trying to stay with Cal was long as possible. He tried to glance over his shoulder at me, but one cop forced his head forward.

For a moment, I saw Cal clench his fists and the muscles in his arms tighten.

"Don't," I said.

His shoulders drooped.

"Come on, Natalie," Mom said, dragging me out by the cloth of my dress. "God, honey, what did he do to you?"

"Nothing, Mom." I tried to look back to Cal, to see where they were taking him. I only captured a glimpse of his head being pushed into a police car before Mom forced me forward.

Once again, they had taken Cal from me.

Once again, he was gone.

CHAPTER 24

Mom can keep me locked up in my room. She can take my phone, she can take my laptop, she can order me to keep my bedroom door open at all times. She can order me to check up with her in the morning, at lunch, at dinner, and when I go to sleep. Honestly? I don't blame her. I've already proven that I'm a sneak when I want to be, that I can escape out my window to run off with my possibly criminal stepbrother.

What she can't stop me from doing is thinking about him.

God, Cal.

I hope you're okay.

My footsteps dragged along the floor as I got ready for school the next Monday. I ignored Mom where she sat at the kitchen table, watching me through slitted eyes and a frown. She still hadn't told me what had happened to Cal. And he hadn't invaded my front bushes and scaled my wall to whisk me away on his motorcycle again, so I was assuming he was being held somewhere.

Possibly a jail cell.

What Mom also couldn't stop me from doing was going to school, especially not now that graduation was only a month or so away. I wished she could. I wasn't looking forward to facing school as "Nat Harlow, the girl who was brought police to prom," even if I had much bigger problems facing me.

And, even worse, I hated knowing what they would be saying about Cal.

I trudged into the school, forcing my gaze to stay forward as I walked to homeroom. I could feel a hallway of eyes on me once again. I hated being the local freakshow. I could stand it when I was with Cal—I loved it when I was with Cal. Even if it was stupid and dangerous, I wanted to be seen with him. I wanted people to know he was mine.

But now I hated it.

And I hated the whispers I kept hearing.

"Did you hear Cal Gatlin kidnapped Nat?"

"I swear to God, he's crazy."

"I heard she's the crazy one now."

"I heard he's still in jail."

I flinched at that last one.

I wish I knew if it was true or not. But Mom wasn't even acknowledging Cal's existence, so I couldn't get much news from that end of the line. And I had a snowball's chance in hell of getting James to let me see his son.

I made through the day before meeting up with Jess at the final student council meeting. Nate was there, unfortunately. But he didn't look at me. He didn't even acknowledge my existence. It was like I was completely dead to him.

Thank God.

"Does everybody … does everybody know? About what happened at prom?" I asked Jess as I slipped into my chair. The meeting had begun and all eyes were on Nate as he rambled on about awards, giving me some privacy for the first time. Even so, a teacher in the corner of the classroom was still tilting her head towards us to eavesdrop while pretending to the adjust the projector.

Ugh. Crashing prom was a bad idea, but I didn't expect it to turn into an infamous one too.

"Well, yeah," Jess said sheepishly. She sat idly scribbled on a small pamphlet on her desk, the order form for our graduation caps and gowns. Three weeks until my high school graduation, and my life was already imploding. Wasn't that supposed to wait until college?

Mom had confiscated my pamphlet as part of her panicked lockdown on my life. I'm not sure what she thought I was going to do with it. Turn it into a pipe bomb, probably. New kidnapper-loving prom-crashing Nat seemed like the pipe bombing type to her.

"Have you ordered your graduation dress?" said Jess, glancing up from her pamphlet.

"No."

"So you're wearing Maneater?" She grinned while glancing at Nate. He droned on, still ignoring me.

"No."

"Because…?"

"Not going."

"For God's sake, Nat. You don't have to be so overdramatic. You're allowed to live a little, even if your incest husband is in prison."

"He's not—"

"Look," she said, grabbing my hand. The student council meeting continued on behind us, Nate still ignoring us as we snuck out of the room. I grabbed my bag and followed her, frowning at the carefree way she flipped her hair. "I'm just saying. He would want you to be happy, wouldn't he?"

"Actually, I think Nate wants me dead."

"You know I meant Cal," she said, cutting her eyes at me.

"Jess, I can't be happy. Not if I don't know he's okay."

"It isn't your responsibility to take care of everybody, Nat." She leaned against her locker. "I can see you tearing yourself down again. You're allowed to feel sad. You don't have to be strong all the time. You're not a bad person for not being perfect."

"That's not what this is about. This is about Cal."

"And he can take care of himself. Have you seen those muscles? The boy could beat a bear. And then the bear would apologize."

"Jess." I could feel a smile creeping onto my lips. I couldn't help but feel better when she was around.

"Besides," she said, perking up at my grin. "He's probably having a great time in jail. Making friends with his own kind and becoming a toilet wine connoisseur? He's Cal Gatlin, the tattooed bad boy with a motorcycle and a reserved place on the FBI's Most Wanted. Jail is his Disneyworld."

"Jess," I groaned.

"You know I'm only trying to cheer you up, Nat."

"I know." I rested my head on her shoulder. It felt good to have someone to lean on for once instead of carrying it all myself. "And I appreciate it. But, God, Jess. I don't know what's happened to him. I don't know where he is. No one will tell me. It's ... it's killing me."

Jess pulled me into a hug.

"This sounds like a job for Ben and Jerry," she said, patting my hair. It reminded me of the feel of Cal's fingers pulling through my blonde locks. My heart warmed.

"With sprinkles?"

"All of the sprinkles. And gummi bears." She gave me another squeeze and pulled out her car keys. "Meet me at my house in twenty minutes?"

"Mom will kill me if I sneak out."

"I'll call her from the school's office phone. I'll tell her it's a graduation practice or something. Very mandatory." She put on her serious business face, and I laughed.

"Thanks, Jess."

"Go get your bike," she said, pushing me away. "You're so slow, I swear!"

I smiled until the ghost of Cal's voice rolled over me.

Come on, Pink. You're so slow.

I shook the memory out of my mind and raced to the parking lot to collect my bike. No more Cal, at least as long as I could do nothing about it. And no more moping. Moping wasn't going to save either of us. Focus on the gummi bears, Nat. Jess, ice cream, sprinkles. No more crying.

By the time I found my bike and had wheeled it out to the parking lot, I had almost forgotten about Nate.

Almost.

"Hey there, Nat."

I froze in the parking lot, my hand clenched on my bike.

No. Not again.

"I thought you were at the Student Council meeting?" I said through gritted teeth.

Nate stood before me, his arms crossed and a cocky smile on his face. I couldn't see anyone around us. We were alone, it was starting to get dark, and my psycho ex had cornered me.

Perfect.

"Saw you leaving, Nat. Couldn't let my girlfriend go out at night alone. You never know how dangerous it could be." He gave me wide puppy dog eyes, completely devoid of emotion.

"Not your girlfriend," I choked.

"Come on, Nat. Don't be like that."

For some reason—namely that I am an idiot—I guess I had assumed he had given up. After all, that's the only reason he would bring police into this, right? He had ruined my life by taking Cal from me. He had "taken revenge" on Cal by putting him in jail. He had gotten back at both of us. He had ignored me in school. There was no reason for him to keep stalking me.

But then again, like Cal had said: Nate was crazy.

And crazy is dangerous.

I turned to him, willing my expression to stay still and hard. My icy gaze glared a hole into him. Bitch Nat was back, and she was angry as hell. If looks could kill, Bitch Nat would be Ted Bundy. My hands balled into fists.

"What do you want?" I spat.

Normally, when someone scowls and growls at you like a deranged bitch, the sane person will back off. But apparently no one had given Nate the memo. Then again, he wasn't sane.

He smiled and took a step forward.

"Come on, Nat. Don't be like that. You know how much I've missed you, don't you?"

"Don't you dare come near me."

"I've missed you, Nat. We were so good together."

I glanced back at the school. There were still a few people milling around in the front lawn, but they were so far away that they were only fuzzy little ants. I doubted they could see my horrified expression. And, worse, I doubted anyone would hear me if I screamed.

Damn this school and their isolated parking lots. It's like they wanted students to be murdered by their stalkers.

"Nate, I swear to God." I took an involuntary step backward as he advanced on me. "I'll scream."

"They won't hear you."

"I'll tell everyone how crazy you are."

"They won't believe you."

He reached for my hand. I yanked it back so hard I nearly fell on my ass. Stop, Nat! Focus! I couldn't afford to make mistakes like this.

"I just want to talk, Nat!"

"Bullshit."

He took another step towards me. I tried to grab my bike, but he tore it out of the way, sending it skidding across the asphalt. My breath caught. He was too strong. It was strength I remembered. Anger strength. Strength that brought the stinging back to my skin where he had hit me.

No, no, no.

Out of the corner of my eye, I could see a figure dressed in sparkly purple slip through the doors of the school. Jess. But she couldn't hear me yell, not yet. The more the situation sank in, the more I realized how utterly fucked I was. If Nate was crazy enough to attack me at school, it meant he was desperate.

And a desperate Nate was dangerous.

My hand darted toward my front pocket, where I kept my mace on a rhinestone keychain.

Nate grabbed my wrist before I could jerk it away.

"Come on, Nat," he growled, forcing me to him. Jess was still too far away, and it had gotten completely dark by now. There was no way she could see us. There was no way she could save me. "We need to talk, baby."

Oh God. His car was there. The door was open. And I was being dragged toward it. A scream erupted from my mouth as I scratched his face.

"Fuck!"

Nate kicked my leg from under me, and I fell helplessly backwards. His hand covered my mouth, and he yanked my arm behind me.

"Come on, Nat," he growled. "Don't be like that."

I bit down on his hand.

Nate let out a strangled growl and pulled his hand back. Another scream ripped through my throat. I saw Jess's head turn from where she stood under the parking lot light. She had heard it, but she couldn't see us through the darkness. Even if she could, there was no way she could get to me in time.

Nate struggled to wrap his arms around me again, but now that I knew how much danger I was in, I was fighting for my life. I thrashed against his arms, biting and scratching whatever I could. My teeth sunk into his shoulder, and I tasted blood.

"You little bitch!"

His heel hit my calf, and there was a loud snap.

Oh, fuck. My leg. I stumbled backwards and fell on my ass, no longer able to stand. Years of lacrosse practice had given Nate powerful legs, and years of laziness had made mine weak. I tried lifting it again, and an agonized whimper escaped my lips. Splinters of pain shot out from the broken bone.

"Not so fucking tough are you now, Nat?"

His fist connected with my face, harder than it ever had hit me before. I went blind as the asphalt bit my cheek. My throat choked and gasped, desperate for the air that had been knocked out of my lungs. He grabbed me by the arm and forced me up, nearly ripping my arm from its socket.

I gasped through the haze of pain as Nate dragged me to his car. I couldn't scratch his eyes out with a twisted arm. I couldn't run with a broken leg. My mace was rolling away from me down the hill of the parking lot. There was nothing I could do but try to fight through the white hot pain blinding me.

All hope was lost.

Until that moment.

"I told you already," a voice growled from behind us.

Nate's head whipped around. He recognized the voice too. Deep. Gravely. Protective. I desperately fought through the haze of pain and darkness, searching for him, unable to believe it. It couldn't be him. It couldn't.

"Don't. Fucking. Touch her."

It couldn't be.

But it was.

My lips parted as Cal emerged from the darkness.

CHAPTER 25

"No."

Nate's voice was a harsh whisper. I desperately searched through the bleary pain that blinded me, hungrily running my gaze over Cal's furious face. It was him. He was back.

And he was furious.

"You're supposed to be gone," Nate choked. "They fucking jailed you. There were fucking cops there, you're not supposed to be—"

A sickening cracking sound sounded by my ear. Nate's grip released me, and I found myself falling to the asphalt again.

I rolled, avoiding another bloody scrape down my cheek. But I was still blinded by the pain and pulsing purple bruise Nate's fist had given my temple. My twisted arm was screaming with pain, and my leg was useless. I laid gasping on the cold ground, the sweat rolling down my forehead in thick droplets. Cal launched himself at Nate, leaving me helpless on the parking lot's wet asphalt.

But somehow, in the delirium, I was happy.

Cal. Cal is back.

Cal came back for me.

His words rang in my ears:

"I will come back for you. No matter what. No matter how long it takes. No matter how hard it is. I will always fucking come back for you, Natalie Harlow. Because you are worth it."

I forced my burning eyes open, desperate to see him again. Nate was bloody and bruised in his hands, and the sickening crunch reverberated off the asphalt as Cal punched him again. There was a crazy fire in Cal's eyes. Another punch, launching Nate's limp body to the ground.

This wasn't protecting me. This was revenge.

He had let Nate win the last fight for my sake. But not now. Not like this. Threaten Cal, and Cal wouldn't care.

Threaten me, and Cal would kill you.

Cal's foot hit Nate's stomach with a force strong enough to burst an organ. Oh God, he really was going to kill him. I tried to stand again, but I collapsed against the ground. Even if my leg wasn't broken, the pain wracking my body crippled me.

"Cal," I rasped.

He hesitated. Only for a moment. When Nate stretched out a desperate hand to drag himself away, Cal launched himself forward again. A sharp kick to Nate's head sent him rolling with a strangled groan. Cal's voice growled threats as he pulled his victim up against for another punch.

"Cal!"

Another sickening crunching noise.

Nate's body went limp.

The sight of large spotlights being turned on filtered through the bleary, blinding pain in my head. I winced against them. There were voices yelling as they approached us, and the sounds of footsteps slapping against the damp asphalt. A purple sparkle caught my eye—Jess. People were coming. But all I could focus on was the stomach turning sound of Cal's fists beating into Nate as he growled, "Don't you ever fucking touch her."

A footstep landed near my face. I felt a hand roll me over onto my back, and I hissed a gasp as the pain shot through me again. Someone's warm palm cupped my cheek.

"She's hurt!" their voice cried.

Someone yelled something at me. Their face was only inches from mine, but I couldn't see anything but a blur. The blooming bruise on my cheek was forcing my eyes shut.

I heard a scuffle as a blurred crowd surrounded Cal. Men's voices yelled, and I saw one thrashing blur that might have been Cal fighting against someone's restraining embrace. Nate's unconscious body was dragged across the parking lot by another group of people, highlighted by a flashlight beam that turned hideously red against his bloodied skin.

"Cal," I gasped one more time.

The commotion stopped. Cal's footsteps halted and he lowered his fists, finally listening to me and hearing the command in my voice. No more fighting. No more violence. No more pain. Not for my sake or for his.

The crowd closed around him. His head turned, and he looked at me for the first time. He moaned.

"Oh, God, sweetheart."

The hand on my face was pressing against the bruise growing across my face, and I winced.

"Don't," I hissed.

"Shit, sorry Nat!"

"Jess?"

The blur above me bobbed their head. I recognized the fuzzy dark brown halo around its face as her curls. Her warm hands pulled the damp clumps of hair out of my face. My stomach heaved when the smell hit me. It wasn't the rain that had made them damp—it was clotting blood.

"Jesus, Nat, are you still alive?"

"Broken leg," I moaned.

"Broken everything, Nat."

The blur shook her head. A few other figures approached, and I felt hands pull me upright. I think I was sitting, but I wasn't sure. My head rolled over to rest on Jess's shoulder. The sounds of growled yells and scuffling bounced off the asphalt from where Cal was being wrestled away from Nate's body. Blood seeped from my hair and cut face into Jess's clothes, and the stains bloomed in thick patches. I wanted to apologize, but I couldn't think straight enough to speak. Jess's arms held me tight to her.

"She said she has a broken leg," Jess said. More hands all over me. Someone grabbed my elbow, and my twisted arm shrieked in pain. I hacked out a guttural moan.

"Careful!" Jess snapped.

"Jess. Cal."

"Not now, Nat! Jesus, you're bleeding out."

"Cal. Go … go get … ow."

"Where is the nurse? Is she still here?" Jess's voice called. I heard the snap of a first aid kit. A cool wet rag was pressed to my forehead, and drops of bloody water rolled down my face.

"Where … where is … Cal …."

"Somebody get her a butterfly bandaid, I think she needs stitches. No, here on her head." A finger pressed into the cut where my cheek had bitten the asphalt. "At least to stop the bleeding."

I loved Jess. She was good at handling emergencies. But sometimes, she was too good. This wasn't girl scouts. And I needed to find Cal before something horrible happened.

I forced my eyes open. Blood filled them, blinding me with red. Cool water was poured out from a water bottle into my face, and I blinked them open again. The bruise was pressing against my eyes, blocking my vision. Jess's face loomed over mine, her face panicked and concerned.

"Nat? Nat, can you hear me?"

Cal was being led away. They were going to arrest him again. They were going to arrest him for saving me.

"No," I moaned.

"Wait, you can't hear me? Or you can?"

I stretched out a hand toward the figure of Cal, wincing against the pain in my shoulder.

"Cal!"

His head turned towards me. His face was agonized. I could feel the pull between us. He ached to come to me as much as I ached to have him here. But I also knew he wouldn't fight with the men restraining him. Not if it would cause trouble for me.

Stupid, selfless idiot.

"Make them stop," I moaned at Jess.

Her eyes stayed fixed on my face as she ran her fingertips over the wounds, like she hadn't heard me. A droplet of salty sweat fell from her forehead onto my lips, and I spat it off. Even that was a struggle. I could feel myself growing weaker.

"Jess!"

"Nat," she groaned. "It's fine."

"It's not fine…" I slurred. "They're going … going to … he didn't start it, Jess! Not his fault…." A heavy, warm drowsiness was pulling my eyelids down and slowing my breaths.

She pinched my neck hard, bringing me back to consciousness.

"I swear to God, if you die on me, I'll kill you."

"I'm okay. But Cal—"

"Nat," she said, taking my chin in her hands and pulling my face close to hers. My crossed eyes managed to right themselves and focus on her face, letting me see clearly for the first time since I'd fallen. "Listen to me. People saw."

"What?"

"People saw, Nat. They know he didn't start it. They know Nat attacked you. They know Cal saved you. Okay? He's not going to jail." She paused. "Probably."

"Jess!"

"I mean definitely! Definitely not going to jail. Okay? Now quit wiggling, I've got to put some antibiotic on this cut."

"How ... how could they see? Too dark...."

"Right. Except the school has security cameras that are can see in the dark." She nodded toward the roof of the school. I had never noticed them before, and I could barely see anything right now let alone tiny cameras a couple hundred feet away, so I took her word for it. "It was how I knew something was wrong."

"You knew?"

"Duh, Nat." She rolled her eyes and dabbed a soaked cotton ball over my cheek. I winced as the sting of rubbing alcohol flooded over my wounds. "I was in the office calling your mom, remember? They keep the camera monitoring stuff there. I couldn't see a lot, but it wasn't hard to figure out what was going on."

"So … so…."

"So Cal is fine. We've got video proof to back it up."

I collapsed in her arms, no longer fighting.

Cal is fine.

Thank God.

"Is he okay right now?"

I tried nodding towards where I had heard him, but I couldn't summon the strength to move my head. Her fingers pressed my head down, forcing me to stay still as she nursed my wounds. Her frown was still stern, but the panic had evaporated from her eyes. I was going to be okay.

"He's in trouble. But he's fine."

"How much tro—"

"Nat, for God's sake, stop worrying. You're fucking bleeding out on the school parking lot with a broken leg! Would you please care about yourself for once? And—oh, thank God! I thought you'd never get here!"

Another blinding flood of light washed over me. Footsteps crunched against the damp gravel around my ears, and I felt strange new fingers running over me. Fiercer stings of pain shot through my body as a damp rag of rubbing alcohol was wiped over my cuts. Latex gloved hands felt around my twisted arm, and new voices began muttering to each other.

"What—" I started.

"EMT, Nat." Jess's warm hand patted my hair. When it pulled away, it was stained deep red. "You're going to be fine."

"But Cal—"

I couldn't finish the sentence. Jess was being pulled away from me. The strange voices were hitting me with a barrage of questions, and I could hear the faint sounds of a police siren approaching. My breath caught as I was lifted onto a stretcher.

Hazy blurs filmed over my vision as I went cross eyed, and a heavy pain weighed my limbs down. The heavy, slow throbbing of my heart worked desperately like it was trying to wade through molasses.

My eyes began to close. I hadn't realized how tired I was.

I caught a snippet of what one of the men in the navy uniforms was saying, something about an ambulance and a hospital. The icy air of the ambulance bathed me in chills as I was slid into place inside. More fingers probed my wounds.

"I'll follow you there!" Jess's voice shouted behind me.

It was the last thing I heard before I blacked out.

CHAPTER 26

"Oh, honey."

My mom's voice was the first thing I heard when I regained consciousness. My eyes fluttered open.

A ringing reverberated in my ears, and my tongue was dry, begging for a sip of water. Aching muscles and the pounding in my head weighed me down in the hospital bed I found myself in. The cold, sterile air of the blue-green room around me bit my tender skin, and the smell of rubbing alcohol stung my nose.

I glanced down at my arm. Needles and an IV were taped to the veins. My head went woozy and my stomach turned.

"Is she awake?"

Jess's voice. Jess was here. And Mom?

But something else, too. I was forgetting something. Something important, and I couldn't remember it for the life of me. I couldn't think straight with the pounding in my head drowning out all clear thought.

I turned my head, blinking against the blurry light.

"Yes," Mom's voice said as her cool fingertips traced lightly over my forehead, brushing strands of loose hair out of my face. "I think so. Nat, can you hear us?"

"I can't move."

What am I forgetting?

"I know, honey. They need you to keep still or else the needs and things will … well…."

She plucked at the IV.

"You'll be fine though, hon."

"No. I mean." My dry, rasping voice scratched at me as I tried to force out the words. I cleared my throat. "Hurts."

"I know, Nat." Jess's voice again. Her face popped into my line of vision, hovering above me as her brunette hair tickled my nose. "But the doctors said you'll be fine. Well, aside from the leg thing."

Ugh. The leg thing. I glanced down, allowing a few seconds for my still hazy vision to focus on me.

Oh.

Oh no.

"They put me in a cast?" I moaned.

"Better than having the wound seal crooked." Mom's lips were pursed in a frown, but it was quivering. She was trying not to smile. "It will be fine. You'll only need it for a month or two. Your graduation gown will cover it."

"Oh God, graduation." My head fell back onto the pillow. "I can't graduate like this. I can barely move."

"I told you, Nat," Jess said, rolling her eyes exaggeratedly. "You'll be fiiiine. You've got a broken leg and a purple face and all you care about is that they made you wear a cast? You're such a drama queen, I swear."

"Purple?" I yelped.

"Oh." Jess grimaced. "Probably shouldn't have said that."

"Where? Somebody give me a mirror." I struggled to sit up. My limp muscles screamed in pain, and the needles wiggled in my vein in a horrible unnatural way. A Velcro restraint latched my wrist to the bed. I groaned.

"Definitely shouldn't have said that."

"Why am I in a straightjacket?"

"Natalie, honestly," Mom said, glancing up in a heaven-help-me way. "It's just to keep your arm still. You move a lot."

"I'm purple?"

"You're fine, Nat."

I expected that to have been Jess's voice, but even through the disorientation induced by whatever they were pumping into my veins, I could tell it wasn't.

Too deep. Too gravely. Too manly for a brunette cheerleader with a purple bedazzled cell phone.

"Cal."

I struggled against the Velcro restrains, needles, and aching muscles to see him where he leaned against the wall in the corner of the room. Jess's hand grabbed my head and forced it back onto the pillow. I glared at her.

"Evening, sweetheart."

His voice. His gorgeous, wonderful, deep, delicious voice. His amazing, not-in-jail, not-on-death-row-for-beating Nate voice. His I'm-here-and-I'm-not-leaving voice.

Wait, evening?

I glanced out the window and groaned.

"How long have I been out for?"

"Twelve or so hours."

"Twelve?"

"Could have been days with that head trauma," Jess said, poking my temple. A sharp burst of pain soared out from the bruise there, and my face screwed up. Jess bit her lip. "Sorry."

"You have terrible bedside manner."

"I know." She flipped her hair. "That's why I'm going to be a wedding planner and not a nurse, duh."

Wait, I'm forgetting again, aren't I?

Cal!

My head struggled to move, but a strong warm hand cupped the back of my head and soothed it. That musky, masculine Cal scent washed over me, drowning out the sterile taste of the hospital's air. Fingers combed through my hair.

Cal was back. He was here.

"You're not ... you're not in trouble?"

"No." His voice was gorgeously warm, washing over me like a hot bath after a night stuck in a snowstorm.

"Video, Nat." Jess gave me a god-you're-so-stupid look. I was getting a lot of looks lately. "I told you. They caught the whole thing on the school's security camera. Do you ever listen?"

"Jessica."

Mom put a hand on Jess's shoulder and pulled her back into her white plastic chair, her stern mama bear voice back on. Cal's fingers continued to stroke through my hair, gently massaging me back into calmness. One finger lingered near my ear to brush over the diamond stud. Still there.

"And Nate?" I asked, closing my eyes.

"Expelled."

"What?"

My eyes popped open. There was no way.

Jess's maniacal smile glowed across her face as she bobbed her head, her hair bouncing along with her.

"Yep," she chirped. "They kicked his ass out."

"Jessica."

"Mrs. Harlow, he beat your kid." Mom winced, but stayed silent. "I think I can cuss when it comes to him."

"Not in a hospital."

Jess groaned. Mom just patted her knee. But Mom's eyes stayed fixed on my cast, and I remembered the bit about the purple face. My body was sore and bruised enough to be a corpse, but I hadn't realized just how bad it was until that moment. A cast on my leg. A field of swollen cuts along my cheek. An entire body of throbbing, burning muscles.

I glanced around at the bare, fluorescent-lit room.

He put me in a hospital.

Jesus.

"He's been arrested. He can't hurt you anymore."

Cal's voice again. I turned to him and drank in the sight of his face. God, I had missed it.

"And he's probably going to be charged with kidnapping and attempted murder, how crazy is that?" Jess said, bouncing in her seat like she was announcing the latest juicy gossip about Vanessa Miller. "You should have seen his face, oh my God."

A smile broke through my cracked lips. Only Jess could make me laugh at her ridiculousness on my deathbed.

"Jessica," my mother hissed.

"Mom, it's fine." I stretched out the arm that wasn't held down by Velcro, testing the twisted arm. It still worked, thank God. "I'm fine. At least I think so."

I paused.

"What about Cal? He's still not in trouble for … for 'kidnapping' me, is he? Or for the fight?"

"We're taking care of Cal." Mom's face had steeled, and she was back to the wonder woman she had been when Dad was dying. The take no shit and kick asses while wearing lipstick and heels kind of woman I had always looked up to. "You don't need to worry about it, honey. Worry about getting better."

"What about James?"

I knew I was revealing too much. I wasn't supposed to know about how terrible he was, and I especially wasn't suppose let Mom know that I know.

But I wasn't going to let this go. Cal had saved me. Now it was time to save him.

"I'm eighteen, Nat." Cal's palm cupped my cheek. The warm, soothing skin felt glorious against my wounds. "I'm an adult, or at least a legal one. I don't have to stay with him anymore. And now that I'm about to graduate, and he doesn't have to pretend to care about me, well...." He shrugged. "He doesn't want me. And I don't want him. It's a clean break."

"But where are you going?"

"He's staying with us." Mom's voice. And it was back to the take no shit, laying down the law tone. She crossed her arms and tipped her chin up. "He saved you, Nat. I'm not going to throw the boy who saved my daughter out on the street."

"Can I join the family too?" Jess said. "I could totally be your favorite daughter. I'm way friendlier than Nat. And I can do nails."

"Jessica," my mother groaned.

"You're going to live with us again?" I said, straining my neck to look up at Cal. His fingertips gently pressed me back onto the pillow, and he smoothed my hair. I knew I shouldn't strain myself, but I couldn't help it. Inside, I was gasping for him. I needed him as much as I needed air to breathe.

"Only if you want me."

I wanted to scream that I would always want him, but that wasn't the smartest thing to do at the moment. At least not in front of Mom. I wasn't sure if she had figured out yet about the 'incest husband' thing, but I wasn't pushing it. If she knew that Cal carried around condoms in his jacket and that we had had a lot of fun with said condoms, she'd have us both in chastity belts locked tighter than Fort Knox.

Cal could do a lot of interesting things with his tongue, but I doubted even he could maneuver through that.

"Yes," I said instead, clasping his hand. His arm rested next to mine, warm and comforting, as vital to me as the IV.

I was desperate to keep him there.

But the soreness in my limbs had started stinging like a bitch. And apparently that had been expected, as a nurse walked in and warned Mom that it was time for another round of sedatives. I groaned in protest, clutching Cal's hand to me. Mom sighed and squeezed my knee above the cast.

"I'll stay the night, honey. Just listen to the doctors and do what you're told. I'll be in the cafeteria if you need me."

She grabbed Jess by the sleeve and dragged her out with her, smart enough to not trust my hypercurious friend alone in a room full of strange medicines and chemicals.

"Cal," I moaned as the nurse began adjusting my IV.

He shook his head as he smoothed my hair down. "I need to go too, Nat. Rules are rules. And you know how much of a stickler for rules I've always been." He flashed me that cheeky smile, the one I loved. My fingers traveled along the stiff stubble of his chin to the diamond in his ear.

I felt a sudden wave of drowsiness wash over me and glanced at the nurse, who had finished with the IV.

"I don't want to be apart again."

"We're still together, Nat," he said, touching my diamond. "I'll just be in a different room. You need some alone time."

"I hate being alone," I slurred. My eyes were closing against my will, and my breathing slowed. Whatever they were pumping into me was strong enough to down a horse.

"We'll talk later, sweetheart," he said, kissing my forehead. "You need sleep. Not to keep worrying about me."

"No," I gasped. The drowsiness was pulling me down like a rip tide, the waves of sleep threatening to drown me. My inner swimmer was slowly succumbing to the dark, warm embrace of the current rising around it. "Cal, I need you."

"I'll wait outside the door for you to wake up."

"But I need you."

"And you have me, Nat. But you also need sleep. You know I want to stay with you, but it's not what you need right now. I'll still be here, sweetheart. I'll always be here."

The ocean of sleep had finally started sucking me down. I struggled against it as I watched him leave, my inner swimmer thrashing against the waves that crashed around me. I needed Cal. I needed his lips, his hands, his fingers through my hair, his everything. I hated to see him go, even if I knew it was the right thing to do. My whole soul reached out for him as he left.

But as it turns out, true love is still no match for medical grade sedatives. My vision began to haze out.

I collapsed in sleep the instant he closed the door.

CHAPTER 27

"Which one does this go to?" asked Cal, holding up an embossed letter with gold edging.

'CONGRATULATIONS ON YOUR ACCEPTANCE' was printed in bright red letters across the front of the pamphlet. We sat at my kitchen table examining the pile of final contenders almost a month after the parking lot incident. My crutches were leaning against the table as we picked through envelopes and colorful letters, all of them sporting the word ACCEPTED.

Cal pretended to examine this particular letter with distaste, but I saw the ghost of a smile cross his lips.

He was proud of me.

That meant a lot.

"Harvard," I said, sipping my tea and slipping another acceptance letter into the pile. My graduation cap and gown were still slung over the chair I had thrown them on an hour ago. I was still getting texts from Jess inviting me to the grad after party she was throwing, with plenty of suggestive pictures of cute boys she had wrangled into attendance.

I glanced out the window. By now, it was ten at night, but I could still hear firecrackers and pop music playing in the street as the graduation parties raged on. Maybe I would visit, if only for a few minutes. It was our graduation night, after all.

Then I glanced down at my leg—still not fully recovered. Jess had not helped by scribbling my phone number and "FOR A GOOD TIME CALL" on the back of the cast. I had only been barely able to cover that with my graduation gown. I definitely couldn't hide it with just a party dress, and there was no telling how many of those wrangled cute boys had been told to look out for cast girl.

Nope. No partying for Cast Nat tonight.

"Are you sure you don't want to go out?" Cal asked me, placing Harvard's acceptance letter into the pile. "Technically we both graduated, even if they didn't let me walk the ceremony. Maybe it would be good for both of us."

"Ugh. No. My head is killing me."

I rubbed my temple with two fingers, wincing against the slight bite of pain. The bruise had mostly gone down by now, and I thankfully hadn't needed stitches. But I did have to take my graduation pictures sporting a massive purple stain across my face, not to mention a cheek so covered in cuts and bruises I looked like the newly reanimated Bride of Frankenstein.

Cal still said I looked beautiful.

"You go," I said. "I shouldn't ruin your big night. After all, it's a miracle you managed to graduate. Didn't you skip the entirety of your sophomore year?"

He rolled his eyes and clasped my hand.

"You know there's no point in being anywhere if I'm not with you, Nat."

"Stop being cute."

"Make me."

He held me hand to his mouth and kissed my knuckles.

"Anyway," I said, slipping the Harvard letter's envelope into my purse, "I'm not the partying type. The last thing I need with this headache is more alcohol.

Not like I can dance, either." I placed my casted foot up in the chair next to me and massaged the aching knee above it. "Besides, do remember the last time we went to a party? Not doing that again. Getting the cops called on us isn't my idea of a good time."

He smiled. "I think I know another way we can celebrate."

My heart fluttered.

"Oh?"

He grabbed my hand.

"Come on, Nat. I've got something to show you."

I glanced back toward Mom's bedroom. She had collapsed in bed as soon as we got home, drunk off the cheap box wine we celebrated with. And probably from the triumphant exhaustion that came without sitting through graduation on edge and hoping desperately that Cal didn't set off a fire alarm or streak.

He had been a good boy, though. Now that he was out from under James' thumb, a lot about him had changed. I hadn't seen anger in his eyes at all. I hadn't seen him close himself off from anyone. He had even told a joke to Officer Furst at graduation, and if that wasn't one of the signs of the impending apocalypse, I wasn't sure what was.

"I don't know," I said, rubbing my cast, nodding towards Mom's room. "She's still not happy with the idea of me going out, even if she forgave you. And with this cast…"

He kissed me.

"Do you trust me?"

I looked at him helplessly.

I sighed. "Alright, fine. But get my crutches. I always end up running when I'm with you."

"That's okay, sweetheart." That dangerous, cheeky Cal smile came back. "No more running. Or crutches. I'll take care of all that for you."

"Cal, don't!"

I couldn't fight him off. And even if I could, I didn't want to anymore. He picked me up out of the chair, slinging me over his shoulder as always. My cast bumped into his chest, but he touched it tenderly, making sure that nothing was hurt.

He patted my ass.

"Come on, Nat. Let's go have fun."

"Right. Fun." I huffed from my undignified position. "Getting carried off like war booty is completely fun."

"Well, fun for me," he chuckled, kissing the top of my thigh where it brushed against his stubble.

My eyes rolled as he carried me out to his bike. I had gotten used to being manhandled by now.

Riding was a little bit harder with a cast. But by now, I fit so perfectly into Cal's body that it didn't matter. I rested my chin on his shoulder as we rode down the dark highway, enjoying the light breeze kissing my bruises and the warm pulse in Cal's neck. We pulled off onto a country road after a while, and the smell of fresh dirt and damp leaves blew over me.

"Where are we?" I asked as we passed a thatch of blackberry bushes. I had never been to this part of town. It was right outside the city. Just close enough to be easy to get to, but just rural enough to be mysterious and new.

"It's a secret, Sis."

"Ugh. Don't call me that."

"Sure thing, Pink."

I glared at him. He felt it from behind him and chuckled.

"Sorry, Nat. You're so cute when you're mad."

"I'm not going to dignify that with a response."

"You just did."

I stuck my tongue out at him.

Ten minutes later, Cal parked the bike behind a thick bush that smelled of sweet, musky flowers. His warm fingers covered my eyes. "Don't look until I say so. It's a surprise."

"Cal, I'm wearing a cast," I groaned.

"I'll lead you. Just trust me."

"Cal."

"I could carry you again."

Before I could protest, he had swept me up into his arms like a princess again. His lips pressed against my temple. "Now don't look, or you'll make me sad."

I squeezed my eyes shut so hard it hurt.

The crunch of twigs and dead, damp leaves under Cal's foot were the only indications that we were moving. I snuggled my face into his neck, inhaling that delicious Cal natural scent as we walked. His strong hands placed me on my feet after a moment. I wobbled on my casted leg, getting my balance.

"Ready?" he asked.

I nodded.

"Open your eyes."

An involuntary gasp escaped my lips when I did.

Bella Scully

CHAPTER 28

Cal had taken me to a small clearing I hadn't known existed. Even now, standing in the middle of it, I wasn't sure it was real. It was a secret garden out of a fairy tale.

A sweet green lawn rolled out before us in shades of emerald and olive, illuminated by dew that clung to each blade and reflected the moonlight. Dark greenery and newly blooming spring flowers hung in thick bouquets around us, gleaming as they reflected the full bright moon and sparkling stars of the clear sky. Dimly glowing lights flashed in the distance from where the city began on the horizon. The heady scent of the honeysuckle and damp ivy swallowed us.

My lips parted, and I stood there in shock. I had never known a place could be so beautiful.

"Do you like it?" he asked.

I nodded.

"My mother used to take me here, sometimes."

"This place? It seems a little out of the way."

"Do you see that hill?" he said, nodding to a small black figure to our side.

I squinted through the darkness. At first, it looked only like another large bush of flowers and ivy. But underneath, I could make out the decomposing bones of some abandoned building.

Charred wood and decayed planks rotted underneath the climbing plants, and I could make out the dull shine of a bronze doorknob under a thick clump of honeysuckle. Shards of broken window glass glittered with dew and moonlight as they littered in front of the old structure. Even though it was old enough to have been reclaimed by the forest and consumed by weeds, I could still smell the fresh sting of sweet mold and ash that wafted from the old wood.

"It was my home as a kid," Cal murmured.

"It burned down?"

"When I was eight. Mom died."

"Oh." I glanced down at the oddly random clearing we had stumbled into. So this would have been Cal's childhood backyard. "I … I never knew how your mom passed away. I guess I assumed…"

"That Dad did it?" He nodded sharply. "I don't blame you. Even at school, people talk about…."

He trailed off.

Of course. Everyone in this town had heard the rumors about Lily Gatlin being beaten to death. I guess the reality was less glamorous. Though I had always heard that it was Cal who had done it, and I realized he must have heard that too. The thought made blood rush to my ears and my fists clench.

Worse, I wanted to collapse in on myself as I remembered what I had snapped at him so long ago, back when I bought into the rumors. The memory of standing in my doorway and hating him fiercely rushed back to me, making me sick.

I want to spend time with my little sister, Sis.

Why? I had answered. So you can beat me to death like you beat your mom?

"I'm sorry," I whispered.

"She couldn't get out in time. Dad had dragged me out already, but she didn't know that. She went back in looking for me. The firemen pulled her out after an hour or two. They wouldn't let me see her." The lump in his throat was wavering. "The smell of burnt hair still makes me sick."

"I'm so sorry, Cal."

Crickets and cicadas chirped around us as we stood in silence. The dew had begun soaking my cast.

"I'm sorry for taking you here, Nat," he choked. "I know this isn't the way you want to spend your graduation night."

"Cal, it's okay."

"But I needed you to see. I needed you to know…." His voice was strained. "I need you to see that this is what I am. People are right about me. I'm fucked up, Nat. I'm the son of an abusive man and a dead woman. I only barely graduated tonight, and that's mostly because they don't want to put up with me anymore. And now that Dad's left me, this is all I have. A burned down house, and no money, and enough baggage for a Delta airline flight. This is what I am."

"I don't care about what you are. I care about who you are."

"Nat," he groaned. "I don't need your mom's cutesy little proverbs. You need to really look at me."

"I am looking, Cal. And I love you."

His eyelids slid shut. "Nat. You're not listening."

"I don't care, Cal. Not about the dad, not about the mommy issues, not about the rumors. So other people don't like you. So fuck them. I know the real you. And I love him."

"It's not just rumors. I do have issues. And you know that, Nat. You saw the way I acted when I got my hands on—" His voice cut off. He couldn't even say his name. He groaned out a strangled sigh. "I hated you seeing me like that. And I hated seeing it myself. I don't want you to have to worry that that's what I'm going to turn into. Girls like you don't deserve guys like me. You deserve better."

"You're not your father, Cal," I murmured.

"But what if I am, Nat?" His head dropped to his hands, and raw pain laced his groaning voice. "What if he's always been there inside me, waiting for the chance to come out? What if that's who I am—a man who beats unconscious people in a parking lot? I would have killed him, Nat. You saw me."

"He would have killed both of us."

"That doesn't make it okay."

"You never hurt me."

"But what about everyone else? I've hurt so many people, Nat. You don't need to hit someone to hurt them. You don't need to beat someone to destroy them. Dad showed me that."

"Cal, listen to me."

I took his face into my hands. His eyes were still sealed closed in pain, but I ran my thumb along the thick eyelashes, and they fluttered open. His eyes searched mine, desperate.

269

"I see you, Cal. The real you. Just like you've seen the real me. I know you're fucked up. I'm fucked up too."

My face nuzzled into his neck, and his arms wrapped around me again. His fingers dug into my side, crushing me to him.

"But maybe we can be fucked up together. Maybe we can save each other. Maybe it doesn't matter that we're fucked up because we've found somebody who can fix us. Maybe that's what love is."

"Life isn't a fairy tale, Nat."

"I didn't say it was one." I glanced up at him, and he pressed his warm lips to my forehead. "But maybe we can make our own."

His face nuzzled my hair, and I sighed contentedly.

"You deserve a happily ever after, Callum Gatlin."

"So do you," he murmured.

"Good. It's agreed, then," I said, straightening up. My cast was damp with dew, and my fingers reached down to adjust it. "We can find a gingerbread house and a couple of German kids to cannibalize, and we'll be good to go."

"Natalie?"

"Hm?"

"Kiss me."

I turned around to see him. His eyes smoldered under his hooded lids, burning into me. My heart jumped into my throat.

Oh, Jesus. I loved it when he looked at me like that.

My heart throbbed in my chest as I pressed my lips to his once more. His tongue slipped between them hungrily. This wasn't one of the lingering, sweet kisses he gave me. This one was urgent. He needed me.

His fingers carressed my jaw as we kissed, the other hand cupping the curve of my breast. I leaned into him, allowing my body to find its natural place against his as he laid us down on the soft grass. God, he smelled good.

"You taste amazing," he breathed.

"You smell nice."

He furrowed his brow, studying me with a puzzled look. A deep chuckle rumbled through his chest.

"You have some strange ideas about sweet talk, Nat." He brushed a strand of hair out of my face, tracing my cheekbone with his thumb. "But I've got to be honest. I kind of like it."

"I aim to please."

He kissed my forehead. "Would you like to just lay here and do a little stargazing? Or do a little more?" His fingers crept between my legs and massaged my inner thigh.

"More, please," I breathed.

His lips pressed against mine, his tongue caressing its way into my mouth again. The weight of his body pushed mine onto the bed of moss beneath us. I ripped the t-shirt off over his head and dug my nails into the bare flesh his back. He hissed in pleasure.

The memory of his scratches at prom and Jess's smirking about our midnight getaway came back to me. A laugh bubbled up out of my chest.

"Honestly, Nat. I'm not that bad at fucking you that you have to start laughing before we even get started."

"No, it's not that."

"Then what?"

"I love you."

He rolled his eyes. "Glad you think loving me is so funny."

"No. I mean…." I bit his lower lip softly. A delicious groan passed his lips. "I really love you. A lot."

"Do you have any idea what you do to me?" he asked breathlessly.

"Yes."

"Then don't you dare fucking stop," he whispered.

The thin sweatshirt I had been wearing was peeled up and over my head, leaving me breathless on the ground with nothing between my naked chest and Cal's hungry gaze. His mouth dove forward, latching onto my right breast. Whimpers escaped my lips as his tongue ran along my nipple, and he sucked hard on my bare flesh.

"Cal," I moaned, threading my fingers through his hair.

"Don't stop," he growled, moving to the other breast. "Don't you ever fucking stop saying my name, Nat."

His fingers fumbled with the zipper of my jeans as his tongue worked over my nipple, tasting every inch of my skin. He yanked my jeans down, and his rough palms cupped my ass. His tongue trailed down my stomach, stopping to dip in my navel before continuing down. His thumbs dug into the soft flesh of my thighs as he spread them.

"Fuck, Natalie. Do you have any idea how gorgeous your pussy is?"

"Please," I begged.

His teeth nipped my thigh. His tongue crept between my legs, and it flicked over my clit teasingly. My back arched.

"Cal!"

"Jesus, Nat. I will never get used to how good this is. How good you are."

I wanted to respond, but the fingers that had slipped inside me were too distracting. They shook as they stroked me from the inside, teasing my walls with a come hither motion. He was trying to go slow for me. But he needed me. He needed me almost as fiercely as I needed him.

His tongue slipped against my folds, and I grabbed at the moss beside us, desperate to hold onto something as he turned my world upside down. The flat of his tongue ran along my clit. He sucked hard on it, drawing out the shudders from my spine.

"Cal," I moaned. His tongue lapped against me mercilessly as his strong hands held my thighs open for him. My hips grinded against his face, desperate for release. "I need you."

He buried his face between my legs. The stubble on his face scraped against my soft inner thigh as his tongue worked against my clit. Deep groans escaped his lips and vibrated against me, driving me closer to the edge.

"Fuck, I need you," he growled, pulling back. His hands reached for his zipper. His cock throbbed in his hand as he pulled it out, swollen and desperate for me. His lips fell on mine again as his cock pressed against my entrance.

"Soft and slow? Or hard and fast?" he panted.

"Hard."

His hips slammed into me.

The feral sounds of his growls and my desperate panting drowned out the crickets and cicadas around us. His hips pounded me into the ground over and over again, no longer holding back. My mouth pressed against his throat, kissing it hard until I could feel the throb of his pulse beating against my lips. His fingers clutched my hips so hard that they left small red marks in the pale flesh.

"Fuck, Nat…. So fucking good…."

"Don't stop!"

His palms cupped my ass again and lifted it, and the next thrust buried him deeper in me than he had ever been before. My hair fanned out behind me as my head tossed back in ecstasy. Deeper and deeper, he pushed himself inside me. He was hitting a new spot now, something sweet and deep inside that drove me so close to the edge that I would fall at any moment.

"Cal," I choked in warning.

My eyes squeezed shut. Yes, yes, yes.

"I've got you," he whispered into my hair. "Just let go."

I couldn't resist him. Not after that. My back arched against him with a helpless moan, and my orgasm crashed over me. White hot electricity coursed through my body to every fingertip and edge, setting me on fire with need for him. My shaking hands and thighs clung to him as he thrusted into me over and over again, his rhythm drawing the orgasm out longer.

I was still panting and gasping for air when he came.

We laid there in each other's arms in the afterglow, his fingers combing through my blonde curls as we watched the stars. My nose nuzzled its way into his neck again, and I inhaled that musky, masculine scent that was uniquely Cal's. I was home again. Finally. And no one would ever take him from me.

"I love you, Nat," he whispered into my hair.

"I love you."

"I think you're right," he said, pulling me closer. "I don't know what will happen to us. I don't know if I'll ever deserve you. But I think you're right. I think you've saved me."

"I think we've saved each other."

"As if you need saving," he said, his lips smirking against my hair. I felt the soft vibration of his deep chuckle. "You would have done fine without me. You always do."

"Yeah, well." I punched his arm lightly. "At least you make things fun. And I've gotten to know the local police really well since you came along."

Another chuckle rumbled through his chest.

God, he was sexy when he did that.

"Come on," he said, looping an arm around my waist. He swept me up in embrace for one last kiss, holding my cast delicately against him. His heartbeat pumped against my chest, throbbing with mine as if we were one person. I smiled against his mouth. I never wanted this to end.

His green eyes twinkled as they gazed into mine.

"Let's go make our happily ever after, sweetheart."

And we did.

ABOUT THE AUTHOR

Bella Scully is the author of steamy, thrilling romance serials and novels. Her debut novel, SAVE ME, was published July 1, 2015. A native of Texas, she currently resides in Austin.

———

For updates, announcements, and more information, you can visit her official website at **www.bellascully.com**

You can also reach her at her email address: **authorbellascully@gmail.com**

———

You can follow her online at:

Facebook (personal):
facebook.com/bellascully

Facebook (official):
facebook.com/authorbellascully

Twitter:
twitter.com/bella_scully

Goodreads:
goodreads.com/bellascully

1028

Made in the USA
Lexington, KY
07 October 2015